PRAISE FOR
THE INCORRIGIBLE CHILDREN OF ASHTON PLACE

"It's the best beginning since *The Bad Beginning* by Lemony
Snicket and will leave readers howling for the next episode."
—*Kirkus Reviews* (starred review)

"How hearty and delicious. Smartly written with a middle-grade
audience in mind, this is both fun and funny and sprinkled with
dollops of wisdom (thank you, Agatha Swanburne). How will it
all turn out? Appetites whetted."

—ALA *Booklist* (starred review)

"With a Snicketesque affect, Wood's narrative propels the drama.
Pervasive humor and unanswered questions should have readers
begging for more."

—*Publishers Weekly* (starred review)

"Jane Eyre meets Lemony Snicket in this smart, surprising sat-
ire of a nineteenth-century English governess story. Humorous
antics and a climactic cliff-hanger ending will keep children
turning pages and clamoring for the next volume, while more
sophisticated readers will take away much more. Frequent plate-
sized illustrations add wit and period flair."

—*School Library Journal* (starred review)

Also by Maryrose Wood

THE INCORRIGIBLE CHILDREN OF ASHTON PLACE

The HIDDEN GALLERY

by MARYROSE WOOD

illustrated by JON KLASSEN

BALZER + BRAY
An Imprint of HarperCollins*Publishers*

Balzer + Bray is an imprint of HarperCollins Publishers.

The Incorrigible Children of Ashton Place Book 2: The Hidden Gallery
Text copyright © 2011 by Maryrose Wood
Illustrations copyright © 2011 by Jon Klassen
Library of Congress Cataloging-in-Publication Data
Wood, Maryrose.
    The hidden gallery / by Maryrose Wood ; [illustrations by Jon Klassen]. — 1st ed.
        p.   cm. — (The incorrigible children of Ashton Place ; bk. 2)
    Summary: Fifteen-year-old Miss Penelope Lumley, a governess trained at the
Swanburne Academy for Poor Bright Females, takes the three Incorrigible Children of
Ashton Place to London, England, and learns they are under a curse.
    ISBN 978-0-06-236694-8 (pbk.)
    [1. Governesses—Fiction.   2. Feral children—Fiction.   3. Orphans—Fiction.   4. Blessing
and cursing—Fiction.   5. London (England)—Fiction.   6. England—Fiction.]   I. Klassen, J.,
ill.   II. Title.
PZ7.W8524Hid   2011   2010032737
[Fic]—dc22   CIP
                                                                               AC

Typography by Sarah Hoy and Dana Fritts
15 16 17 18 19   CG/OPM   10 9 8 7 6 5 4 3 2
❖
Revised paperback edition, 2015

For my two incorrigible siblings, Thomas and James.
We were not raised in a forest, but we did
live among the Woods.
—M.W.

After an hour's aimless wandering she knew
that she and the Incorrigibles were lost . . .

THE FIRST CHAPTER

*A fit of pique encounters
a bit of pluck.*

"BUT THE WORKMEN *SWORE* THE repairs to the house would be finished by now!" The blushing pink circles that typically adorned the cheeks of Lady Constance Ashton were now as scarlet as two ripe nectarines. "I fail to see how three mere children, no matter how Incorrigible, could do so much damage. Just thinking about it makes me feel perilously close to having a tantrum!"

"It appears that Lady Constance is in high dudgeon," Miss Penelope Lumley thought to herself, as she stood just outside the doorway of the lady's private parlor. "Perhaps I ought to come back another time."

As you may know, "dudgeon" is a word that describes feeling cross, and to be in high dudgeon means feeling very cross indeed. (Do not be one of those careless speakers who says "dudgeon" when they mean "dungeon." Being locked in a dungeon might well cause a person to be in high dudgeon, but that is the only real connection between the two.)

"Dudgeon" is the sort of old-fashioned term one rarely hears nowadays, but the condition it describes remains all too familiar. Only an exceedingly fortunate, patient, and sweet-tempered person can go through life without ever feeling in high dudgeon, and that was just as true in Miss Penelope Lumley's day as it is in our own.

To be sure, most people would consider Lady Constance Ashton exceedingly fortunate: In addition to being young and pretty, she was married to the vastly wealthy Lord Fredrick Ashton and was thus the mistress of a great house full of servants (including the head housekeeper, Mrs. Clarke, who was the unlucky person now being scolded about the house repairs). But no careful observer was likely to accuse Lady Constance Ashton of being patient and sweet tempered.

Penelope certainly would not. On the contrary, she

found Lady Constance's frequent tirades rather wearying. Penelope was only fifteen, yet even she could see such behavior was ridiculous, and Lady Constance was a married woman of nearly twenty! And this habit of blaming the three Incorrigible children for all sorts of things that were simply not their fault—at least, not entirely—was vexing, to say the least.

Besides, Penelope had been standing at the door of Lady Constance's dressing room for a quarter of an hour waiting to get a word in, and her feet were beginning to ache. If she were not able to make her request soon and get back to the nursery for a cozy read-aloud in a comfortable chair with her three attentive pupils gathered 'round, she might be in real danger of slipping into high dudgeon herself.

"I'm sure the workmen are doing their best, my lady." Mrs. Clarke was a sturdy sort of woman, stout in both build and character, and yet there was a wobble of fear in her voice as she answered her mistress. "Do keep in mind, it is a very old house, and when you fix one thing, something else is likely to fall apart as a result. Why, who was to know that hanging new drapes in the parlor would cause all the plaster around the windows to crumble into dust? Or that sanding the scratches out of the floorboards would show them to be full of termites? Or that scrubbing the wine stains from the antique carpets would cause such dreadful holes to open up? Or—"

"Excuses, excuses, *excuses*!" Lady Constance shrieked. "Next you will tell me the house is cursed! Oh, my head! Bring me a cold compress, please, I am quite at my wit's end—and some tea—and a chocolate, quick! Make it a whole box!"

"As you wish, my lady." Mrs. Clarke backed out of the room with remarkable speed. Indeed, she had huffed and puffed her way to the end of the hall at a full trot before Penelope even had a chance to catch her eye and offer a look of sympathy.

Lady Constance clutched the edge of her vanity, panting with distress. It was not an ideal opportunity to beg a favor, but "She who waits for the perfect moment to act will never make a turn at a busy intersection," as a very wise woman named Agatha Swanburne once remarked, so Penelope forged ahead.

"Pardon me, Lady Constance," she said, in the same soothing voice she used to calm the Incorrigibles when they were in the presence of a small, tasty rodent, or during a full moon, or when they had gotten worked up over a particularly thrilling bit of poetry (Penelope's three pupils were not, strictly speaking, ordinary

4

children, but more on that later). "May I have your permission to speak? I have a small request to make, and it requires a timely response."

"A timely response, you say? A timely response? That is *precisely* what I cannot seem to get! Since Christmas Day my home has been all but uninhabitable, and all I ask for is a timely response! *When* will the repairs be finished? *When* will the workmen be gone? *When* will the hammering and clattering be over? The noise—the dust—the smell of turpentine—"

If you have ever ridden on a tire swing after turning the rope 'round and 'round until it was twisted from top to bottom, you will have some idea of the wild, spinning, escalating whirl of Lady Constance's distress. "And Lord Fredrick is so blasé about the whole thing! 'All in good time,' he says, in that indifferent way of his, but of course he is at his club more often than not, so nothing that goes on at Ashton Place troubles him; why should it?"

"I am in receipt of a letter," Penelope pressed on, for she had no desire to hear about Lady Ashton's marital woes, or anyone else's for that matter. "It is from Miss Charlotte Mortimer, my former headmistress at school."

Suddenly worn out from complaining, Lady

Constance slumped in her chair. "School?" she mumbled. "What school? Ah, you mean that Swanbird place; what of it?"

Actually the school was named after its founder, the aforementioned Agatha Swanburne, but in the interest of time Penelope let the error pass. "Miss Mortimer will be visiting London soon, and wishes to know if I might meet her there for a brief visit. I have not seen her in some months—ever since I was hired as a governess here at Ashton Place, in fact—so it would be a great pleasure to call on her. I would bring the children with me, so they would be no trouble to the household during my absence. And, of course, you may deduct the time from my pay, if you wish."

Penelope added this last bit about docking her salary because she knew it was the type of argument that Lady Constance found persuasive, but privately she thought it would be rather unfair for the lady to take her up on it. Whether they were in London, Budapest, or Timbuktu, she was still the children's governess, after all. And just think of all the educational things they might do in a big city like London! There would be libraries everywhere, and theaters and museums, parks and palaces—why, it was like something out of a book!

In fact, it was all out of books, for Penelope had never been to London. However, she had read a great deal about it: a noisy, odorous, fogbound city where gaslight made the nighttime bright as day, yet the air was so thick with coal soot that the daytime was dim as dusk, and where poor orphans were likely to have terrifying encounters with escaped convicts, but were just as likely to inherit large fortunes willed to them by long-lost relatives they never knew they had. Surely such a paradoxical place would be well worth a visit.

And to see Miss Mortimer! That would be best of all. Penelope felt she might even grow misty eyed to be reunited with her much-loved and much-missed teacher and friend. It was possible Miss Mortimer would shed tears of joy as well, for among all the many penniless, intelligent girls at the Swanburne Academy for Poor Bright Females, Penelope had always been a favorite of hers.

The thought of her kind but stern headmistress made Penelope stand up a little straighter herself. "Lady Constance, I would like to post a reply to Miss Mortimer at once, since she will need time to arrange our travel and lodgings. May I have your permission to make the trip?"

Lady Constance's head was buried in her hands.

Her muffled voice emerged through her fingers, one strained syllable at a time.

"London . . . lodgings . . . lodgings in London . . . Lumley . . . London . . . brilliant!" She lifted her head. Her circular, doll-like eyes shone with a strange, mad glee. "Miss Lumley, you have provided the perfect solution to my dilemma!"

"Does that mean we may go?" Penelope readied herself to curtsy and bolt from the room in search of pen and paper, for it was coming on two o'clock; the serving man who brought the mail to town left at half past, and she was determined to get a letter out to Miss Mortimer that day if at all possible.

"It means, Miss Lumley, that we shall *all* go!" Lady Constance flew to her feet and chasséd giddily around the room like a tipsy ballerina. "I will have Lord Fredrick lease us a suitable house in London. Nothing elaborate—the finest house in Kensington will do, furnished with all modern comforts and a few priceless antiquities, of course—and we shall live in town and enjoy ourselves like civilized people until this wretched place is inhabitable again."

Her pale hands flew up to cover her mouth. "Whoops! I know I should not say Ashton Place is wretched, for that is disrespectful to Fredrick, not to mention his poor ancestors, all of whom died such gruesome deaths—but you know what I mean."

"I am not sure that I do." Penelope could not tell whether Lady Constance's sudden notion of relocating the entire household was excellent news or the worst possible turn of events. "Do I understand you correctly, my lady? You mean that you and Lord Ashton and the children and I, all of us, will go to London? And stay in a house that Lord Ashton will arrange?"

Lady Constance was no longer listening. "Naturally, I shall bring a dozen or so servants from Ashton Place with us. Any halfway respectable house will no doubt come with a staff, but one can never have too much help, and I like to have familiar faces around me. Although I daresay I will not be at home much, once my presence in the city is known! I have many, many friends in London. So does Fredrick, though I find most of them tedious, especially that awful Baroness Hoover—something about her makes my skin positively crawl—but enough of that! I must write and let everyone know we are coming. It will be an endless round of luncheons and teas and parties. And shopping, of course!"

She tossed her head until her butter yellow ringlets bounced like springs. "Really, it will be so marvelous to be in town. I may decide not to care if those awful workmen ever finish fixing the house at all. And it is all thanks to those dreadful Incorrigible children!"

Penelope dipped her head to hide her embarrassment. Alexander, Beowulf, and Cassiopeia Incorrigible were her pupils. That is what Lord Fredrick had named them; what their original names were no one knew, since they had been found wandering naked and howling in the forest. To all appearances, the trio of barking, nipping, squirrel-chasing imps had been raised by wolves, and this was why they were not, strictly speaking, ordinary children.

Alas, the memory of how the three Incorrigibles had behaved—or, to be accurate, failed to behave—at Lady Constance's holiday ball was all too fresh in Penelope's mind.

"Indeed, my lady," she said meekly. "If you will excuse me now, I shall write Miss Mortimer at once and tell her the happy news."

But, much as a soufflé comes piping hot out of the oven taut and round as a birthday balloon but shrivels disappointingly as soon as the cool air hits it, her own mere mention of those "awful workmen" had already caused Lady Constance's enthusiasm to collapse into a fresh fit of pique.

"Awful, clumsy, incompetent workmen! I shall have them all fired," she fumed. "Even better, I shall have them arrested for disturbing the peace. They are a disturbance to the peace of my home. Miss Lumley, you must ring for a constable, quickly!"

Now, recall that Penelope was quite anxious to make the afternoon post. She was also reluctant to have people arrested for no good reason. Therefore, she now proceeded to do something quite rare and brave—something you yourself may find it necessary to do someday, if you have not already had cause to try it out. In short, she stood up to a person of authority in high dudgeon.

"Respectfully, Lady Constance, I will do no such thing." Penelope spoke in her best kind but stern voice, just as Miss Mortimer would have done. "It is a very inconvenient situation, to be sure. But the workmen have been trying their best, and surely that is all one can ask of them."

Lady Constance turned and faced Penelope, hands on hips. Her dress was a cream-colored parfait of flounces and bows, but her expression, so gay and animated a moment before, was now furious and tight-lipped. She looked like an ill-tempered wedding cake with feet.

11

"I have noticed, Miss Lumley, that you are inclined to be *optimistic*." At the word "optimistic," Lady Constance crinkled her nose in the manner of a person detecting a bad smell. "It is a most unfortunate habit, and I sincerely wish you would stop."

"I will do my best," Penelope said with a curtsy. As she made her exit from Lady Constance's chamber, in the privacy of her own thoughts she added, "Yet to think I might actually stop would be foolishly optimistic on my lady's part!"

It was quite true. Optimism, and persistence, and the knack for getting impossible tasks well in hand, despite false starts and mishaps—a useful mix of traits best summed up by the word "pluck"—had been at the very heart of Penelope's education at the Swanburne Academy for Poor Bright Females. It was nearly a year since she had graduated from that worthy institution, but by now pluck was part of the young governess's nature, and that was unlikely to change anytime soon.

For, no matter where fate, happenstance, or wanderlust might carry her, Penelope was a Swanburne girl, through and through.

THE SECOND CHAPTER

*The children carry things
a bit too far.*

WHEN LADY CONSTANCE SAID THAT the condition of
Ashton Place was "all thanks to those dreadful Incorrigible children," she was referring to the events of
the previous Christmas, only a few months prior. That
is when Alexander, Beowulf, and Cassiopeia, after
being asked to perform a *tableau vivant* for the guests
at Lady Constance's elegant holiday ball, managed to
make an absolute wreck of the house while in hot
pursuit of a runaway squirrel. The whole time they
were dressed in their new party clothes, which were

also, unfortunately, ruined.

How a squirrel ended up smack dab in the middle of the dance floor was unknown. Mrs. Clarke thought the dim-witted rodent may have simply snuck in through an open window, but Penelope suspected foul play, for there had been some strange goings-on at the ball that seemed purposely designed to work the Incorrigibles into a frenzy: a series of entertainments based on the theme of wolves, for example (which, Penelope discovered afterward, had been commissioned by someone who bore the initial A).

But the fateful appearance of that mayhem-inducing squirrel was the topper. The children had chased the pint-sized troublemaker all the way upstairs, only to discover faint, mysterious howling sounds emerging from a secret attic room, the door to which had been camouflaged beneath some rather tasteless wallpaper.

Penelope puzzled over these mysteries daily, and had even paid a surreptitious visit or two to the attic while the children were otherwise engaged. There she heard nothing unusual, although she was by now quite familiar with the strange, dark forest scene that was painted on the wall.

The mural itself had been damaged in spots by all the wallpapering done over it, so she was not able to make out the artist's signature. However, after consulting some dusty books of art history she found in Lord Fredrick's library, she concluded that it was a third-rate example of the Ominous Landscape school of painting, which had never quite caught on with critics or the general public and had been quickly superseded by other, less depressing styles.

That this particular Ominous Landscape featured the terrifying figure of a wolf, yellow eyed and with fangs that dripped blood, was one more disturbing mystery to add to the pile. It was all rather unsettling to think about; in short, it would be a relief to get away from Ashton Place for a while—and to London! What a marvelous adventure that would be!

Back in the nursery, Penelope gathered the children 'round and told them of Lady Constance's plan. She fully expected their excitement to match her own, for who would not feel a thrill to visit London, home of Queen Victoria and Prince Albert, capital city of the nation, seat of the empire, and (one might argue) the cultural and economic crossroads of the world?

Cassiopeia, the youngest Incorrigible, looked up at Penelope with her green, pixieish eyes.

"Nutsawoo come, too?" she asked sweetly. "To Londawoo?"

Penelope had not thought of this. Nutsawoo was the very same squirrel that had caused such a ruckus at the holiday ball. Somehow the furry scamp had avoided being torn to shreds by the children and had subsequently become Cassiopeia's beloved pet, living on the tree branches outside the nursery windows. Having already given such glorious chase in pursuit of him (or her—Penelope was not entirely sure how one told the sex of a squirrel, and was not inclined to investigate), the children had grown more or less immune to Nutsawoo's "squirrelyness" and could coexist calmly with the anxious little creature. Alas, this privilege did not extend to others of Nutsawoo's kind. To the Incorrigibles, they remained fair game.

Cassiopeia gazed pleadingly at her governess, waiting for an answer. What to do? Nutsawoo could not come to London; that was obvious. But how to convince Cassiopeia? The child was quite attached to her twitchy, beady-eyed pet.

"The city is no place for a squirrel," Penelope began, but then thought better of it, for of course the many parks of London were no doubt overrun with squirrels.

"Nutsawoo is not accustomed to travel and might catch cold," she then commenced to say, but again she stopped, for surely Nutsawoo had done nothing his whole life but skitter from tree to tree over the vast forests of Ashton Place. In terms of sheer mileage, he had likely traveled far more than Penelope had, and in all sorts of weather, too.

Beowulf and Alexander flanked their sister. All three children lifted their shining eyes to Penelope, and one of them (she could not tell which) whimpered imploringly. It reminded her of the not-so-distant afternoon when she had first discovered the three siblings locked in the barn at Ashton Place, unkempt, unschooled, and untamed—truly, so much had changed since that day! And yet so much, clearly, had not, for Beowulf was starting to drool in anticipation of her reply.

"Nutsawoo," she said finally, "does not own any appropriate luggage."

The three Incorrigibles looked at their governess as if she were not entirely well. However, Penelope had once taken a class at Swanburne called Great Orations of Antiquity, in which she had to memorize famous speeches given by generals and politicians from days of old. From this exercise she had learned that when faced with the task of having to convince the citizenry of a flimsy argument, the best strategy is to speak in a loud voice and leave no time for questions.

"No luggage. There; that settles the matter," she

bellowed. "Nutsawoo will stay here and keep an eye on the nursery while we are gone. On to geometry! Gather your graph paper, please."

Cassiopeia's eyes began to well up with tears.

"It will be a short trip and the time will go quickly," Penelope added, sounding less firm than before.

"Postcard?" the girl asked with a sniff. "For Nutsawoo?"

Penelope was about to explain that Nutsawoo could not read, but then she sighed. For how could she argue? After all, these were three children who had lived in the woods with no one but wild animals to care for them. If they could be taught, by patient repetition and the judicious use of treats, to live indoors, eat cooked food (liberally doused in ketchup, of course), appreciate the rudiments of poetry, and even perform complicated dance steps, as the Incorrigibles had already, impressively, done, who was to say that dear Nutsawoo, somewhere in the shallows of that simple, frantic squirrel brain, might not appreciate receiving a picture postcard from London? The naughty fur ball might even write back, for all Penelope knew.

"Of course we will send postcards to Nutsawoo. And we shall bring him back a present as well. In fact," she went on, with the instinctive knack every good governess has for turning something enjoyable into a lesson, and vice versa, "I will expect all three of you to practice your writing by keeping a journal of our trip so that Nutsawoo may know how we spend our days. Why, by the time we return, he will think he has been to London himself! He will be the envy of all his little squirrel friends," she declared.

Penelope had no way of knowing if this last statement was true. Could squirrels feel envy? Would they give two figs about seeing London? Did Nutsawoo even have friends? To seriously consider the answers to these questions would require Penelope to do something called "going off on a tangent," which is another way of saying "to stray from the subject at hand." To go off on a tangent is always a risky maneuver, for once one has gone, it is often surprisingly difficult to find one's way back. Penelope knew better than to let this happen, so she simply stood her ground and waited.

Luckily, it took only a moment for her statement about Nutsawoo to have the desired effect on the children.

"Pictures?" Beowulf asked. Beowulf loved to draw and had a real talent for it, too.

"Yes, you may include pictures in the journal." Fearing she was making the assignment too easy, Penelope added, "But the captions must be written in French. Now, that is quite enough discussion, for 'Ten parts talking is half as much as one part doing,' as Agatha Swanburne used to say. Never mind about the graph paper. We shall study geometry by calculating the volume of our suitcases and organizing our packing accordingly."

The children eagerly obeyed and gathered their possessions into neat piles, which they proceeded to measure. Alexander jumped on his pile and knocked it over a few times before settling down to work, and Beowulf had a tendency to gnaw on his ruler, but not to the extent where it threw off his arithmetic. Cassiopeia, though the youngest, was a whiz at math, and easily finished before her brothers.

All the while Penelope heard the three of them murmuring to one another in funny little grunting sounds, which, she assumed, constituted their efforts to learn some French in time for the trip. She hardly expected them to do so, as they were still getting accustomed to expressing themselves in English (as opposed to barks and howls), but the challenge would help keep them occupied and, she sincerely hoped, far away from trouble.

"We shall study geometry by calculating the volume of our suitcases and organizing our packing accordingly."

"I TELL YOU, MISS LUMLEY, it was just like watching one of those Spaniards in the tight suits and funny hats—the ones who get in the ring with a crazed bull and cry, 'Toro! Toro!' while waving a red blankie around." Mrs. Clarke used her large apron (conveniently stained cherry red, since she had recently baked a pie) to demonstrate.

"Toro! Toro!" she exclaimed with verve. "Except this time Lady Constance was the minotaur, and Lord Fredrick was the bull, you should pardon the expression."

"I believe you are referring to a matador," Penelope helpfully corrected. Mrs. Clarke did not seem to pay her any mind. She was too busy relishing her own performance, a dramatic reenactment of the negotiations between Lady Constance and her husband, in which the lady informed Lord Fredrick that he needed to lease a town house in London at once.

According to Mrs. Clarke, the encounter could only be described as toreadorical: the outright threats and faked retreats, the defiant swirl of Lady Constance's red skirts, the snorting, stamping protest of Lord Fredrick. Finally, the cunning matador played dead. Then, when the bull's guard was down, she brandished a dagger to deliver the final blow.

In Lady Constance's case, this meant a heartrending bout of weeping, followed by the threat that she would succumb to something called a "conniption fit" if Lord Fredrick did not agree to her plan that instant. Penelope did not know if a conniption fit was a serious medical condition, but it certainly sounded unpleasant to endure, and even worse to witness.

Lord Fredrick must have thought so as well, for it was quickly decided. A house in the city would be leased, a battalion of servants would be installed, and Lady Constance would be given a generous shopping allowance to boot.

"It'll be a pleasant change of scene for the staff, anyway." Mrs. Clarke was flushed with exertion and excitement. "But if Lady Constance doesn't give alternate Sundays as a half day for the servants, there will be plenty of grumbling among them, mark my words."

"A half day would hardly be enough time to see the sights of London," Penelope began to protest, but she was interrupted by a frightful noise, which seemed to have its origins rather close by.

"Torowooooooooooooooo! Torowooooooooooooooo!"

It was the Incorrigibles. Penelope had been under the impression that they had retired to the back nursery for afternoon naps, or perhaps some quiet activities such as chess (which the boys enjoyed a great deal) or practicing sums on the abacus (a favorite pastime of Cassiopeia's). But in fact they were leaping from bed to bed in a wild game of bullfighting. Alexander had assumed the role of matador, and Beowulf and Cassiopeia were taking turns charging at him. One of the red velvet curtains from the window now served as the matador's blanket.

"Children, stop!" Penelope cried in alarm. "That will be quite enough of that. The poor window curtain! All the loops are torn off. It will not hang up properly again without a good deal of mending."

The children, whose tendency to get carried away was exceeded only by their eagerness to please, looked crestfallen.

"Sorry, Lumawoo," Alexander offered, his head down. The other two made apologies as well, using the socially useful phrases they had studied so diligently. "Deepest apologies! Regretfully yours! Will not happen again!"

"Peculiar, isn't it?" Mrs. Clarke observed, as an aside. "Three savage creatures such as they are, and yet they still enjoy imitating wild animals. You'd think they would've had quite enough of that sort of thing in the forest, where they were raised."

Of course, it was Mrs. Clarke they were imitating, for how would the children know anything about bull-fights and matadors? They would not have been likely to meet any in the woods of Ashton Place. Nor could they fairly be called "savage," not after all Penelope's hard work teaching them. Did savages know their multiplication tables? Did they enjoy the poetry of Henry Wadsworth Longfellow? Could they repeat a few pithy phrases in Latin? Certainly not, and the Incorrigibles could do all those things, after a fashion.

They were, however, prone to mischief, especially when in high spirits. "As are most children," Penelope thought resignedly. "But that is no excuse for destructive behavior."

"Your apology is accepted, children," she said aloud. "Now, let us start tidying up this mess—"

"Mrs. Clarke say, 'Torowoo,'" Alexander interrupted, with the barest hint of a frown.

"And wave skirt," Cassiopeia added, demonstrating with the torn curtain.

Beowulf added nothing further to these arguments, but pressed his lips together unhappily to prevent himself from chewing. The children had apologized, but clearly they also felt that an injustice had been done, for why should they be scolded for playing matador when the housekeeper was not?

Penelope began to explain. "I do realize that Mrs. Clarke was just now imitating a bullfighter, and therefore you must have thought it was a splendid idea and an enjoyable way to pass the time. And it is, certainly, but only within reason. Do you understand?"

The three Incorrigibles looked at one another. It was plain that they did not understand, and who could blame them? "Within reason" is not the sort of place one can easily find on a map; in fact, its location may vary considerably from one day to the next. It was only when Penelope tried to explain such notions to the Incorrigibles that she realized how the precise meaning of "getting carried away," "taking things too far," "going overboard," and other, similar figures of speech were all woefully hard to pin down. Alas, once the room was a shambles, the curtains ripped, and the pillows emptied of feathers, their meaning became all too clear.

Mrs. Clarke also tried to shed light on the matter. "It's true I was saying 'Toro, toro,' but only to describe to Miss Lumley something that happened between our master and mistress. So I wasn't playing bullfighter at all, you see. I was telling a story. It's a whole different business."

"Metaphor?" Cassiopeia inquired.

"Minotaur, silly!" Mrs. Clarke patted the child indulgently on the head. "Aren't you a bright little thing, though?"

Penelope felt the time had come to put a stop to this conversation. "Never mind, children; your apologies are accepted. Now make up your beds, just as they were before you started to play minotaur . . . I mean, metaphor—matador! . . . and fold up the red curtain neatly so I may give it to Margaret to be sewn. If you can get all that done and settle yourselves calmly in your chairs near the hearth within, say, ninety seconds"—she took out a pocket watch to mark the time—"I will read aloud to you."

As the children scrambled to do as they were told (for, like most children, they dearly loved to be read to), Penelope reached into her apron pocket and withdrew a small volume. "My former headmistress, Miss Mortimer, has sent us a guidebook describing all the important sights of London. It should provide us with an excellent preparation for our trip."

"Sights and sounds are all very well, but I prefer a nice lady's hat shop myself," Mrs. Clarke said, with a dreamy look on her face. "And a confectioner's. A bit of money in hand and a half day off on alternate Sundays, that's all the preparation I need."

Whether Mrs. Clarke was truly in need of a confectioner's shop was a matter of opinion, but Penelope was too busy timing the children to comment. "Eighty-eight . . . eighty-nine . . . ninety. Well done! Now, come sit down and let us begin. *Hixby's Lavishly Illustrated Guide to London: Compleat with Historical Reference, Architectural Significance, and Literary Allusions,*" she said, reading off the cover. "What a marvelous gift."

"Ahwoooooosions!" the Incorrigibles howled in agreement. Then all four eager pupils—for Mrs. Clarke secretly liked to be read to as well—gathered 'round to listen.

THE THIRD CHAPTER

*The Incorrigibles travel by steam
engine, with heated results.*

THE *HIXBY'S GUIDE* HAD COME by return post as soon
as Miss Charlotte Mortimer received the letter con-
firming that Penelope and the children would be
heading to London. It was both a practical and a fashionable gift, for at the time, guidebooks were all the
rage, and there were scores of them available on every
conceivable topic: from Audubon's *Birds of America* to
Zachary's *Taxonomy of Badgers, with Their Cubs, Accu-
rately Figured.*

Fans of ferns could choose from among dozens of

best-selling titles, including Frondson's *Pteridomania for the Beginner, with a Preface on Spores by Dr. Ward.* (It should be noted that ferns were wildly popular in Miss Penelope Lumley's day, much more so than in our own.)

As for travel guides, there were Black's *Picturesque Tourist* guides to England, Scotland, and Wales, and Harvey's indispensable *On the Cheap: Touring the Continent on Five Pence a Day.* Few would risk crossing the Atlantic without a copy of Appleton's *Railroad and Steamboat Companion. Being a Traveler's Guide Through the United States of America, Canada, New Brunswick, and Nova Scotia. With Maps of the Country Through Which the Routes Pass, in the Northern, Middle, and Eastern States,* a book whose title was as grand and cocksure as the New World it so thrillingly described.

There were scores of books about London, naturally, but in the note accompanying her gift, Miss Mortimer assured Penelope that *Hixby's* was by far the best of the lot, and she should use no other to find her way around town. As the title promised, the volume was lavishly illustrated with thumbnail-sized watercolor paintings, most of which depicted wildflower meadows and snowcapped mountain peaks. Neither of these seemed likely to be a prominent feature of the city.

However, the pictures were attractive, and Penelope liked them a great deal. She found herself admiring them during the long carriage ride to Ashton Station, where she and the Incorrigibles would soon be boarding the train to London.

"In fact," she told the children as they stood in line to buy tickets, "these miniature paintings are so delightful that I think our very first excursion must be to the British Museum. According to Mr. Hixby"—and here she thumbed her way to the appropriate page—"we are to 'avoid the crowds that throng before the more well-known works, and concentrate on obscure galleries for the discerning visitor.'"

She showed the page to the children so they could admire the illustration (it was a very pretty lake scene). "Mr. Hixby calls Gallery Seventeen, Overuse of Symbolism in Minor Historical Portraits, a 'must-see.'"

"Then we must see it," Alexander replied, and Beowulf yapped in agreement. Penelope corrected him with a glance, whereupon he said, "Yes, we must," just like a proper English schoolboy. Cassiopeia, still sad from her tearful leave-taking with Nutsawoo back at Ashton Place, was silent. She remained so until they were done purchasing their tickets at the ticket window and had walked outside to the platform to wait for their train. Then she began leaping up and down.

"Torowoooo!" she yelled, pointing. "Torowoooo!"

"I doubt you will see any matadors on the train platform," Penelope remarked. "If we were traveling to Spain, perhaps. Or to a costume ball."

But it was the steam locomotive itself that had overheated the little girl's imagination. It was one of the new shiny red Bloomer engines, a flashy piece of engineering and full of pep, too. (Returning briefly to the subject of guidebooks: For technical specifications on the Bloomer, there is no better reference than *Craswell's Opinionated Guide to British Steam Locomotives*. Alas, copies are notoriously hard to come by.)

"Torowoooo!" The boys took up the cry, pointing and jostling each other. "Torowoooo!"

Penelope looked, and although she did not howl "Torowoooo!" like the children, she was just as impressed. The locomotive was a gleaming scarlet, with a forbidding front grille of inky black. Two shiny gold smokestacks rose above. Truth be told, the appearance of the Bloomer was not unlike a black-nosed, golden-horned, bloodred bull, snorting and puffing steam out of its nostrils and its tall, glittering horns.

When the conductor sounded three deafening, mournful hoots on the train whistle, the children

32

covered their ears and howled even more loudly in protest. "All aboard," the conductor cried. "This is the London and North West Railway, eleven oh seven train to London, making all local stops. Final destination will be Euston Staaaaayshun!"

Clutching their second-class train tickets, Penelope helped the children up the steep metal stairs. It was just the four of them; Lady Constance and Lord Fredrick would be driven to London by private coach in a day or so, as soon as Lord Fredrick put his business affairs in order. The servants had gone ahead with the luggage so that they might unpack and prepare the house for the family's arrival.

"Metaphor! Metaphor!" Cassiopeia kept shouting as they boarded the train. The child was doubly mistaken, for in the first place she meant matador, and in the second place there was no matador, just a bright red steam locomotive. But in another—one might even say, metaphorical—way, she was perfectly correct, since a train whisks its passengers from here to there in much the same way that a metaphor carries one idea into another (turning a squabble between husband and wife into a bullfight, for example).

If Penelope had been paying full attention, she might have pointed this out to the children and made a fine lesson from it. But her mind was on a different train ride altogether. "How interesting it is," she mused as she settled the children into their seats. "Ashton Place felt so strange to me when I first arrived here from my familiar, beloved Swanburne, on a train very much like this one. And now Ashton Place is home, and London is the strange new destination."

Then another, related thought occurred to her: What would it be like to see Miss Charlotte Mortimer again? Penelope felt she was scarcely the same person she had been at Swanburne. She was no longer a student; now she was a teacher like Miss Mortimer. She had grown taller and filled out a bit; this she knew from the fit of her clothes.

"Dear me, I hope she does not ask me to call her Charlotte!" Penelope thought in alarm. "It would be terribly awkward, after thinking of her as Miss Mortimer for all these years. Yet I suppose that is how life goes." Penelope closed her eyes, for she felt suddenly drowsy. "New things become familiar with time, and familiar things become strange. It is very curious and"—*yawn*—"tiring to think of."

Already the train was having its inevitable nap-inducing effect. The three Incorrigibles were out cold, nestled in a heap on the seat, and Penelope was ready to follow their example. As the train wheels *clickity-clack*ed along, Penelope's head slowly leaned back against the seat. Her eyelids grew heavy until finally they fluttered closed.

The copy of *Hixby's Guide* began to slip from her loosening grasp. Now it lay in her lap, jostled back and forth with every lurch of the train. From there it would soon fall to the floor with a *thud—*

Grrrrrrrrrr!

Penelope startled awake to behold a most unexpected scene, in which all three Incorrigibles played prominent roles. Alexander's teeth were bared to the molars. Beowulf was growling like a mad thing, and Cassiopeia's jaws were locked on to the sleeve of a man in a long black coat, who was trying unsuccessfully to shake her off.

"I beeg yer pardon!" the man said heatedly. "Miss, could you call uff your cheeldren? The gurl is aboot to draw blood." His accent was hard to place.

"Children, whatever is going on?" Penelope cried.

"Man steal book," Alexander said in a fierce, low voice. His eyes were fixed on the intruder. The fellow was tall and rotund, with a misshapen nose and a hat pulled low over his eyes.

Penelope glanced down at her lap. Her *Hixby's Guide*

was gone. Frantically she looked around the seat and floor. Then her eyes traveled upward to the man's arm, still held fast by Cassiopeia's teeth buried in the coat sleeve. The book dangled between his fingers.

"I will take that back, thank you," she said curtly, snatching the book away.

"It was falling to the floor, miss. I only mint to kitch it and put it on the zeet next to you while you slept," he said in his inscrutable accent. "The flur is so dirty and demp, it would be have been rooned."

"Thank you kindly for your trouble." Out of the corner of her eye Penelope noted that the children were still on high alert. What animal instincts did they have, she wondered, that made them know when danger was present?

"Is ridikalus book in any case," the man pressed on. "Full of mistikes and out of deet. If you like, I will geev you my copy of *Parson's Pictorial Pamphlet Depicting the City of London and Environs, Second Edition,* and tek this worthless tome off your hends."

"A moment ago you were afraid it would be ruined. Now you say it is worthless. I find your arguments somewhat contradictory." Penelope smiled in a way that was not at all friendly; it was a trick she had learned from Lady Constance but had never before had reason

"Man steal book!"

to use. "I thank you again for your trouble. Good day."

"Good day," Alexander repeated through bared teeth; as a result the phrase, while socially useful, was not very well pronounced.

"*Grrrrrr* day," said Beowulf, most unpleasantly.

"Let go of the man's sleeve, dear," Penelope instructed. Cassiopeia obeyed with reluctance. There was a small rip and a half-moon-shaped wet spot in the fabric where her mouth had been. Under different, friendlier circumstances Penelope might have offered to have the coat mended, but these circumstances were not those. Penelope drew the children close to her and regarded the man with what she hoped was a stern and fearless gaze.

The man lingered briefly, as if he would say more. With a parting glance at the *Hixby's Guide*—did Penelope imagine it, or was it a longing, greedy, covetous sort of glance?—he left.

Cassiopeia wiped her mouth on the hem of her dress. A tiny, bright green feather came unstuck from her lips. She held it between two fingers, then blew it into the air. They all watched as the downy tuft wafted hypnotically back and forth, back and forth, until it disappeared under the seat.

"Yukawoo," Cassiopeia remarked before curling up

next to her brothers once more. "Taste like pillows."

The three children quickly drifted back to sleep. Penelope did not. She remained anxiously alert for the rest of the trip, holding tight to her *Hixby's Guide* and ready, frankly, to pounce.

"LONDON, EUSTON *STAAAAAAAY*SHUN!"

"Hold hands, children, hold hands!" The passengers stampeded out of the train like a herd of cows that were late for a very important milking appointment. Penelope clutched her carpetbag with one hand and Alexander's sweaty fingers with the other. Alexander held tightly to Cassiopeia, and Cassiopeia held just as tightly to Beowulf. In this white-knuckled way, the three groggy children and their nervous governess snaked through the crowd, searching for an exit.

Penelope could not help trying to catch a glimpse of the strange man who had tried to steal her *Hixby's Guide*. She did not see him, but in such a large crowd it would have been nearly impossible to find anyone. The thought made her squeeze Alexander's hand so tightly that he yelped.

"It was an unpleasant incident, nothing more," she thought bravely. "I ought not to make too much of it, for pickpockets and rogues are a commonplace in

39

London. We must stay on our toes, that is all."

With that settled, Penelope turned her attention to a more immediate concern: finding her way to Number Twelve Muffinshire Lane, which was the address of the house Lord Fredrick had rented. She knew that London was a large, bustling, and confusing city, and that one wrong turn might send them wandering down dark cobblestone streets that dead-ended at smelly slaughterhouses and riverfront establishments of ill repute. However, there was a foldout map in the back of her guidebook, and the children were skilled trackers—at least when in a forest.

Once the foursome had elbowed their way out of the station, Penelope tried to get her bearings by holding the map open and spinning it 'round until it resembled the maze of streets that crisscrossed before her. The sidewalks outside Euston Station were even more crowded than the interior of the station had been. Passersby jostled Penelope this way and that, making it difficult to keep the book open to the correct page. Not only that, but the foldout map was so charmingly decorated with pretty alpine meadows, it was impossible to read the street names.

"Excuse me," Alexander said pointedly as people kept bumping into them and pushing past, often while making rude remarks. "Pardon me. I beg your pardon."

"I quite agree, Alexander," Penelope said, making a final, futile effort to read the map before putting it away. "There is a distinct lack of good manners on display—yet there is no need to growl quite so loudly, Beowulf. Someone might take it the wrong way."

Penelope was still not entirely sure in which direction they needed to go. Herding the Incorrigibles before her, she moved toward the nearest intersection. Omnibuses hurtled down the street at alarming speed, and a line of hansom cabs waited at the curb. The drivers prowled the sidewalk, angling for customers.

"Need a cab, miss?"

"Where ya going, miss?"

"Give ya a lift, miss? Half fare for the children."

Penelope thought she might have enough money in her purse to pay for a cab, although she had no idea how much they charged, as she had never taken one before. But the drivers seemed somehow menacing to her, with their fake friendliness and huckstering offers of a ride. Perhaps it was some lingering disquiet from that unpleasant incident on the train; she found herself backing away from the line of hansom cabs and clutching the children even more tightly than before.

"We shall walk," Penelope announced to the Incorrigibles. "I am sure it cannot be very far to Muffinshire Lane. And there will be so many interesting sights along the way."

At that moment a gusty wind kicked up and nearly blew the four of them in front of a speeding omnibus. Penelope waited until the wind died down before continuing, this time with one hand holding on to her hat. "As Agatha Swanburne once said, 'Assuming that one is on dry land, the best way to see the sights is on foot. Otherwise, use a canoe.' Come along, children."

Actually, Agatha Swanburne never said any such thing, at least that Penelope knew of. But somehow, pretending that she had made Penelope feel a tiny bit less nervous as she and the Incorrigibles began to navigate their way through the unfamiliar streets.

THE FOURTH CHAPTER

*A bizarre old woman and a
perfectly nice young man.*

IF YOU HAVE EVER HAD the misfortune of getting lost in
a crowded city, you are no doubt already acquainted
with a surprising and little publicized fact: The greater
the number of people who might potentially be asked
for directions, the more difficult it becomes to get
someone to actually stop and help.

Scientists who study human behavior call it the
Who, Me? syndrome. For example, if you should have
the truly awful luck to get a sliver of sparerib stuck
in your throat while dining alone in a restaurant in

which there is only one other customer, your fellow diner, although a total stranger, will almost certainly leap up and start performing the Heimlich maneuver as soon as you make the universal sign for choking. (If in doubt as to what this sign is, please refer to the informative poster on display in the dining area; this is assuming you are still conscious, of course.)

Whereas, if the same incident takes place in a bustling restaurant full of people, by the time you draw attention to your plight you may have already turned blue and fallen to the floor. At that point you are truly in a pickle, for instead of swift action there will be a lengthy discussion as onlookers try to determine which of them is best qualified to assist. Some will suggest mouth-to-mouth resuscitation, while others will strive to recall episodes of medical television dramas that may or may not be relevant to your case. A few will phone for help; others will panic and require medical assistance themselves; and many, alas, will simply be annoyed that their dinner was interrupted and will tip their waiters ungenerously as a result.

Knowing this, in the future you might well choose only to dine in unpopular restaurants. Penelope did not have this option. London was crowded, and there was no getting away from it. Each new street she trudged down with her three weary charges in tow seemed more packed with unhelpful people than the one before. After an hour's aimless wandering she knew that she and the Incorrigibles were lost, but all her attempts to ask for directions went unanswered in the din and rush of the crowd.

Nearing exhaustion, Penelope pulled the children into a dim doorway. There she hoped to catch her breath and make some sort of plan. As it turned out, the doorway already had an inhabitant: a stooped, ancient woman who blended effortlessly into the shadows.

Drawing upon her last reserves of pluck, Penelope addressed the woman. "Pardon me, madam. Do you have any idea where Muffinshire Lane is? I believe there are likely to be fancy shops nearby?" Penelope did not know for certain about the fancy shops, but given Lady Constance's affinity for spending money, she felt it was a safe assumption.

The woman stayed silent. There was something foreign looking about her, Penelope realized: She was dressed in the manner of a Gypsy fortune-teller, with numerous colorful scarves wrapped around her head and a large and equally colorful shawl wrapped around her broad, hunched shoulders. She wore bangle earrings and rings etched with strange talismans on each of her gnarled fingers. Her deep-set eyes were as dark and shiny as two black olives.

"I am sorry to have disturbed you, then." Penelope sounded forlorn. She was tired and cold, and she knew the Incorrigibles must be as well. Worse, she had run out of biscuits. This was a serious concern, for if the children got too hungry she would have a hard time keeping them from stalking the less agile members of the local pigeon population—a messy and unpleasant business she would much prefer to avoid.

The situation was growing desperate, and in Penelope's view that meant that desperate measures were called for. She took a deep breath and addressed the Incorrigibles. "Children, I want you to wait right here. We must get some proper directions at once. I am going to search for a constable to help us. It will be faster if I go myself, but you must promise"—and here she looked at them very sternly—"*solemnly* promise not to move from this doorway."

She turned to the old woman. "I hope it is all right with you if I leave the children here—I trust they will not be in your way?" She was still not sure that the woman could understand her.

But apparently the crone did understand. "No worry, miss. I watch your babies," she replied in a raspy voice.

"Thank you." Penelope heaved a sigh, more of fatigue than relief. "That is very kind of you. I will return as soon as I am able to obtain help. Alexander, you are the eldest—please make sure no one wanders off."

With that, Penelope, with some misgivings, to be sure, but not knowing what else to do, left the three Incorrigible children huddled in the doorway.

"Nice babies," the old woman said, and smiled broadly. She possessed approximately half the number of teeth that one might expect to see in a person's mouth. It was not a comforting sight.

Cassiopeia whimpered, and Beowulf salivated with anxiety. Alexander was just as uneasy as his siblings, but since he had been charged with being responsible, he comforted them the best way he knew how. He grabbed them by the scruff of the neck and gave them a good shake, until they started to yap and nip each other playfully, just as puppies would.

The Gypsy woman took a long, hard, curious look at each of the children in turn. Abruptly she reached into the many folds of her shawl; out came a deck of large, rectangular cards.

"Cut," she ordered, holding the cards out to Alexander.

"Excuse me?" He cast a nervous look in the direction

in which Penelope had disappeared.

The woman demonstrated how to cut the cards and offered the deck to Alexander again. He did exactly as she had done. She shuffled the deck, turned over the top card, and gasped.

"Ahwoooooo," she moaned ominously.

The children were quite taken aback. Cassiopeia started to howl an anxious reply.

"Ahwoooooo?"

But a disapproving pinch from Alexander stopped her. All three Incorrigibles understood that Lumawoo (as they privately called their beloved Miss Lumley) did not approve of them barking and howling in public, if it could be helped.

"Strange babies," the woman intoned. "Wolf babies! Be careful!" She tapped the card with her long, crooked index finger. "The hunter is on the loose." Then she covered the card with her hand and let her eyes roll upward alarmingly, until they nearly disappeared into her skull. "The hunt is on!"

"The hunt—?" Alexander began, but the woman startled, and cocked her head to listen. She quickly stuffed the cards back in her shawl, out of sight. Then she slunk away, disappearing into the shadows as if she had never been in the doorway at all.

"The hunt is on!"

A moment later, Penelope returned. Her step was brisk out of habit, but the news was bad. "There is not a soul in London who can direct us to Muffinshire Lane, it seems," she announced with false cheer. "Apparently we are staying in a neighborhood so exclusive that no one has ever heard of it. Why, children, whatever is the matter? You look as if you have seen a ghost!"

At that they could contain themselves no more. They howled, and howled, and howled again, long and loud and mournful, as if the sky were made of nothing but full moons.

"There, there." Penelope patted their backs in turn. "Were you afraid? Did that old woman leave you here alone? That will teach me to rely upon strangers to babysit, there, there, now—"

"I say!" A young man stuck his head out of a window two floors above. "What's all that racket? Is everything all right?"

"Yes," Penelope called back, but the children were still carrying on in a most frightful way.

"Ahwoooooooooooooo!"

"Ahwoooooooooooooo!"

"What?" the young man yelled down, louder. "Is someone hurt?"

"We are quite all right, thank you."

"What? I can't hear you."

"Ahwoooooooooooo!"

"Ahwoooooooooooo!"

"Ahwoooooooooooo!"

"I'm coming down!" The young man's head disappeared back inside the window. Straightaway there was a great clatter and thumping and the crash of things colliding. From the sound of it, this fellow was taking the stairs two at a time.

"Dear me," Penelope thought in alarm. "If the gentleman files a complaint about the noise, we may end up gaining the attention of a constable after all, though not in the way I intended."

He burst out the door of the building and skidded to a stop. At the sight of him, the three Incorrigibles stopped howling and stared.

"Oh!" he exclaimed, taking off his hat. "You're just children. That's all right, then. Sorry to have shouted. Sometimes the local ruffians set dogs to fighting so they can make a profit off the betting. I can't stand to see it, personally. Let the blackguards bash away at one another, if they must! But dogs are a man's best friend."

Cassiopeia hopped over and licked his hand. Before Penelope could explain and apologize, the fellow grinned and spoke warmly to his new acquaintance.

"You like dogs, too, I see. What's your name?"

"Cassawoof," she said with pride.

"Nice name! I'm Simon." He wiped the back of his hand on his jacket before extending it to Penelope. "How do you do, miss? Simon Harley-Dickinson, at your service. I live upstairs." He jerked his head up toward the window from which he had first made his presence known. "It's a bit downtrodden, don't I know! But that's the life of the starving artist for you."

"I am Miss Penelope Lumley. How do you do?" Penelope straightened her spine and shook his hand firmly. It was not easy to maintain her composure when so many surprising things kept happening one right after another, but she was a Swanburne girl after all, and manners were manners. "Allow me to introduce Alexander, Beowulf"—the boys bowed—"and you have already met Cassiopeia."

"Charmed, I'm sure." The young man shook hands with the boys and winked down at the tiny girl. "Now, what brings you lot down here? This isn't the nicest neighborhood in London, you know. You'd best be on your way home, if you don't mind me telling you what to do."

"I wish you would tell us what to do, actually." Penelope felt suddenly near tears. If this amiable fellow could not help them, she did not know where else to turn. "We are looking for Number Twelve Muffinshire Lane, and we are quite lost. No one has been able to direct us. Do you have any idea where it might be?"

"Muffinshire Lane?" He stroked his chin thoughtfully. "Muffinshire Lane? Doesn't ring a bell, I'm afraid. But don't fret, Miss Lumley. I've a knack for navigation. It's in the blood; the men in my family have been sailors going back generations. Say, do you happen to have a map handy? I bet I can help you sort everything out, if you'll let me have a look."

After a moment's hesitation (for she had not forgotten that unpleasant incident on the train), she handed him the guidebook. "Thank you so much," she said, meaning it most sincerely. "Are you a sailor, too?"

"Me? Not a bit. I write plays. I'm a man of the theater. A bard, if you will. Sorry, I know it sounds stuck-up when you say it like that. But it's true. I may be a bit of a genius, in fact; I do feel a gleam of it here and there. Although, to be honest, I've had a hard time getting words on paper lately." He turned the guidebook over in his hand. "*Hixby's Lavishly Illustrated Guide to London*, eh? That's a new one."

"I was told it was the best guide to the city," Penelope confessed sheepishly.

"Never heard of it," he said, leafing through the pages. "Smashing pictures. Bracingly alpine. Not much help in finding your way about town, though—ah, here's the map. Now let's see about this Muffinshire Lane. . . ."

AFTER APPROXIMATELY ONE QUARTER HOUR of saying "hmm" and "say" and "well" at least a dozen times each, after which he dashed upstairs to his garret to fetch a rather impressive antique brass sextant, and then another quarter hour waiting for the sun to peek through the smoggy London air so he could get his bearings, this perfectly nice young man named Simon knew precisely how to get to Muffinshire Lane.

To Penelope's great relief, he insisted in escorting her and the children; he said it was more or less on his way, since he was not going anyplace in particular, and he feared they would get turned 'round again completely if he left them to their own devices. As they walked he told amusing stories about life in the theater, which made Penelope fervently wish that she and the children might be able to see a show during their stay in London. She had no idea how to get tickets or what they might cost, but she resolved to look into it at the earliest opportunity.

"Muffinshire Lane," he announced, all too soon, it

seemed. "But are you sure it's Number Twelve you're looking for?"

"It is, but my heavens! Is this what passes for a town house in London?" Penelope gazed at the magnificent building before her. After living at Ashton Place she was no longer shocked by luxury, but still—Number Twelve was something to see.

"I'd call it a mansion myself, but then again we bards are used to humble quarters. Say, you're not members of the royal family in disguise, are you? Secret cousins of the queen? Pretenders to the throne? That would be a good plot for a play." He took a scrap of paper and a pencil stub out of one his pockets and jotted some quick notes. "A mysterious young princess, and the three true heirs—of course you're much too young to be their mother, though I do see a resemblance."

"Oh, no! We are far from royalty, and the children and I are no relation." Penelope couldn't help smiling at the thought. "And this is certainly not our house. I am their governess. I am employed by Lord and Lady Ashton, of Ashton Place."

"The Ashtons! Of Ashton Place! You don't say!" He let out a low whistle. "They've got piles of dough, that lot. I mean, piles!"

Penelope did not feel it was proper for her to offer

"Is this what passes for a town house in London?"

an opinion about the Ashtons' wealth, so she merely replied, "You have heard of the family, then?"

"I've heard of their money. Who hasn't? And my great-uncle Pudge used to mention the name now and again. There was an Admiral Ashton who he knew from his sailing days. That's all ages ago, of course."

Penelope nodded, for she had once seen a large and forbidding portrait of Admiral Percival Racine Ashton hanging in Lord Fredrick's taxidermy-filled study. "I believe the admiral was the current Lord Ashton's great-grandfather," she explained. "What a coincidence that your great-uncle was acquainted with him."

"It's a very large sea, to a sailor," Simon answered thoughtfully, "but a small world, to be sure. Say, that's pretty good." He jotted down this bon mot with his pencil nub. (As you may already know, a "bon mot" is a clever saying. Agatha Swanburne would be a good example of someone who was adept at crafting bon mots, but Simon Harley-Dickinson certainly showed some talent in this regard as well.)

Penelope glanced over her shoulder at the stately house marked Number Twelve. She knew it was long past time for her to take the children inside to settle in their new, temporary quarters, to have supper and a bath and a bedtime read-aloud. But she felt in no hurry to go in. And the boys were engaged in fishing a bit of string out of a curbside puddle with a stick. Surely it would be a pity to interrupt them.

"Mr. Harley-Dickinson, if your great-uncle is an old family friend of the Ashtons, perhaps you would care to bring him over for tea sometime?" She made the offer quickly, even recklessly, for she knew it was hardly her place to invite people to tea—yet she found herself grasping for any excuse to have this intriguing Simon person visit Number Twelve Muffinshire Lane again.

"Uncle Pudge, come to tea? Impossible, I'm afraid. He's in the old sailors' home, in Brighton. Not quite all there in his wits anymore, but he's got more wild seafaring stories in that gray head than you could shake a stick at. You're awfully kind to think of it, though."

Simon shoved his hands in his pockets and shifted his weight around a bit, then blurted: "Say, Miss Lumley—do you like to go see shows?"

"I certainly do!" she exclaimed, with a bit more enthusiasm than the question warranted. "That is to say, this is my first trip to London, so I have not had the opportunity to seen any shows before, but, in theory, I believe I would enjoy it very much."

"That's good to know. Theoretically speaking, I

mean." He was still fidgeting every which way. "I'll be off, then."

Cassiopeia, who had not left his side this whole time, reached up and tugged at his arm. "Resembawoo?"

He frowned, confused. "Rezzawot? What's that you say?"

Penelope smiled. "Cassiopeia means that she would like you to elaborate on the comment you made a moment ago, about there being some resemblance between me and the children."

He scratched his head. "You got all that from what she just said? Amazing. All I meant was that the four of you look a bit alike. You've got nearly the same color hair, for one thing."

"Apples," Cassiopeia agreed. By that she meant reddish, although a person who was accustomed to talking about hair would be more likely to describe it as a rich auburn. All three Incorrigibles had that same striking, auburn-colored hair. For as long as Penelope could remember, her own hair had been dark and dull, but in recent months it had begun to take on a similar (and rather more attractive) hue—ever since she had stopped treating it with the Swanburne hair poultice. Come to think of it, all the girls at Swanburne had dark, dull hair. Perhaps the poultice's lice-repelling and scalp-rejuvenating properties affected color as well. Penelope made a mental note to ask Miss Mortimer about it.

"Apples? I like apples, sure, who doesn't? It's very pretty, too. The hair, I mean." Simon sounded bashful all at once. "Good day, then. It's been a pleasure."

"Thank you again for all your help. I hope your creative difficulties are over soon. In fact, I believe they will be," Penelope added on impulse.

"You're very kind to say so. Cheers." He tipped his hat, and was gone.

Penelope blushed. Pretty hair? She was not accustomed to receiving compliments of this sort, especially from persons of the male persuasion. As one might expect, the Swanburne Academy for Poor Bright Females had been woefully undersupplied with boys, and as a result Penelope had hardly met any in her life.

"But if Simon Harley-Dickinson is at all representative of his kind," she thought, with a pleasantly giddy kind of satisfaction, "then boys must be a thoroughly delightful species! I shall have to make it a point to meet more of them, as the opportunity permits."

THE FIFTH CHAPTER

*A pleasant walk turns into a brush
with calamity, and all because of a hat.*

IF YOU HAVE EVER TAKEN a long-awaited journey to
a far-flung destination, you may have encountered a
painful condition known as "holiday fatigue." This
is the phenomenon whereby, after weeks of excitedly
shopping for straw hats and suitable luggage, making
lists of what to pack and what to leave behind, purchasing bug repellent and checking weather reports,
and then traveling by foot, aeroplane, tramp steamer,
hot-air balloon, or what you please, you arrive, finally,
in Mahi-Mahi or Ahwoo-Ahwoo or some other rare

and spectacular locale, only to discover that you would much prefer to be at home.

You have not gone mad. You recall your name perfectly well, know what year it is, and can correctly identify the capitals of at least a few midsized European nations. But your wanderlust seems to have wandered off. The Hawaiian shirts fairly scream to be put on, the sunscreen smells appealingly like coconut—and yet you spend the day in bed, glued to the hotel television. Instead of breaking out the crampons and pickax and scaling the legendarily slippery Mount Crisco, as you had so keenly looked forward to doing, you stumble to the vending machine down the hall to purchase stale candy and a lukewarm soda. Soon, even that pathetic excursion requires more zip than you can muster.

No one is immune to holiday fatigue, and it is contagious: One grumpy traveler can make the rest of his or her party miserable before the station wagon has left the driveway. So far Penelope showed no symptoms. She had slept like a rock in the small upstairs bedroom next to the children's room and awoke refreshed. She spent the early part of the morning happily engrossed in her *Hixby's*, planning her first full day in London in that eager, list-making sort of mood that starts people whistling jaunty tunes without even knowing they are doing it.

The Incorrigibles, alas, were a different matter.

"London no. Go home." Cassiopeia announced when Penelope asked her for the second time to run a comb through her hair.

"But we have not even begun to see London yet," Penelope replied with mild alarm.

"We see London. Too much London. Miles and miles." Beowulf yawned widely. He had already put on his clothes, but his shoes were on the wrong feet, a mistake he had not made for some weeks and that he now seemed in no hurry to correct.

If Alexander had a complaint, it remained unspoken, but that was because he had so far refused to get out of bed. The covers were drawn completely over his face. Only the hank of sleep-mussed hair poking through the blankets revealed his presence.

Penelope did not like the look of this one bit. Thanks to Mr. Hixby, she had devised a highly educational walking tour that would allow her to drop a letter at the post office for Miss Charlotte Mortimer, followed by a brisk ramble through St. James's Park, where she planned to give her pupils a brief lesson in plant identification. They would then proceed to Buckingham Palace, arriving at the time of day when the light would be best for sketching. Afterward: tea and crumpets at an inexpensive café, then a long, looping stroll that would take them past both Houses of Parliament, Big Ben, London Bridge, and St. Paul's Cathedral. Their walk would conclude at the brand-new British Museum, where they would spend the remainder of the afternoon touring the galleries and perhaps pop in on a lecture or two.

It was an ambitious plan, to be sure—in particular, a lecture at the museum might be pushing their luck—but Penelope was raring to see the collection of Overuse of Symbolism in Minor Historical Portraits that the *Hixby's Guide* recommended so highly, and wanted to squeeze it in somehow. And with so many wonderful places to visit, how could any of them be put off until tomorrow?

Penelope thought she had planned the day from top to bottom, but she had not planned that the children would be in a funk, and so, she realized, her plan must be altered. She took a deep breath and said:

"Who wants breakfast?"

All three Incorrigibles perked up slightly at the suggestion, but they were still too grumpy to reply.

"Well, I certainly do." She rose and walked to the door. "I will go downstairs and fetch some. When I return, I expect all three of you to be out of bed, hair combed, faces washed and fully dressed. If you are ready before I return, please practice your cursive letters. I have already tacked a helpful diagram on the wall." This was another example of Penelope's optimism, for the two younger Incorrigibles were sloppy printers at best; Cassiopeia struggled mightily with the spelling of her own name, and even Alexander was prone to mixing up his p's and q's.

Yet Penelope believed that the best approach was to set a high standard and encourage the children to jump for it. It was the way she herself had been taught, after all. As Agatha Swanburne once observed, "When a big leap is required, a running start makes all the difference—so get moving!"

She left without waiting for a reply. Penelope had no idea what she might find in the kitchen; she had not seen Mrs. Clarke, and all the servants were frantically preparing the house for the arrival of Lord and Lady Ashton. "But even if there is no breakfast made," she thought determinedly, "surely a lane called Muffinshire will be equipped with a charming little bakery somewhere close by."

Down the stairs she went, from the servants' and children's quarters upstairs, past floor after floor of parlors and sitting rooms, dark-paneled libraries, and extra bedrooms for guests. There was a whole floor for the private use of the lord and lady of the house, with spacious bedchambers, dressing rooms, and the most newfangled lavatories imaginable, including actual flush toilets and slipper-shaped tubs that could heat up their own bathwater.

Finally she reached the bottommost floor, which was the domain of the cook, the scullery maids, and the laundresses. Although the cook was nowhere in sight, she discovered a big pot of porridge keeping warm on the kitchen hearth. She filled the bowls herself, sprinkled each with cinnamon and sugar, and since she did not know how to work the dumbwaiter, carried the meal all the way back up those many stairs on a tray.

To her great relief, the children were waiting for her in her room. They were dressed, though still looking glum. Alexander had stubbornly kept his blanket wrapped around him like a cape, and no one had taken a stab at the cursive letters. Penelope waited until the Incorrigibles had finished eating their porridge before speaking.

"Wasn't that delicious?" she said, stacking the empty bowls on the tray. "I do so love the taste of cinnamon. Now wash your hands and put on your coats, quick

quick! We have an exciting day in store."

There were whimpers of protest. Penelope paid them no mind. "In the first place I wish to send a note to Miss Mortimer, letting her know that we have arrived in London and are eager to see her. We shall deliver it to the post office ourselves. Afterward . . ." She paused, for even she suspected that her grand scheme for the day might be enough to send anyone scuttling back under the covers. "We shall go exploring," she finished, leaving it at that. "I have devised a walking tour. It will be very educational."

"Sextant?" Beowulf asked nervously. "Astrolabe?"

"No, we do not need a sextant—nor an abacus, Cassiopeia, please put that back." Penelope patted the *Hixby's Guide* with confidence. "Yesterday was a bit of a muddle, but I believe I have the hang of things now. After the post office we will proceed to Buckingham Palace." She thought she saw a glimmer of interest in her three pupils, and added, "That is where Queen Victoria and Prince Albert live, you know."

Under the table, where he no doubt thought he would not be seen, Beowulf quickly switched his shoes around to the correct feet.

"Postcard of the palace?" Alexander asked, letting the blanket fall to the floor.

Cassiopeia leaped up at her brother's suggestion. "Nutsy Nutsy Nuts*awooooooooooo*!" she howled excitedly, and offered Penelope her coat.

"Good girl; think of what we shall write to Nutsawoo. Surely he would be disappointed if we came all the way to London and did nothing but mope about the house."

Penelope felt slightly silly pretending that she cared about Nutsawoo's opinion. "After all, not even Edith-Anne Pevington wrote postcards to Rainbow, clever pony that he was," she thought as she helped the little girl squirm her arms into the sleeves. "But the children's imaginations must be indulged."

(Actually Penelope was mistaken, for there was a book late in the Giddy-Yap, Rainbow! series in which the pony-crazed heroine, Edith-Anne Pevington, did, in fact, send a picture postcard to Rainbow while taking a round-the-world voyage with her eccentric aunt. Alas, *Edith-Anne Takes a Trip While Rainbow Stays Home* was not one of the big sellers of the otherwise popular series, which perhaps explains why Penelope had overlooked it.)

In any case, her new plan worked: Thanks to a hot breakfast, a bit of kind but firm handling, and a helpful (if imaginary) nudge from a squirrel, all three

Incorrigibles had managed to shake off their holiday fatigue and were now ready to venture forth.

As they proceeded to the stairs, Alexander extended his hand to Penelope in an offer to take charge of the *Hixby's Guide*. "Knack for navigation," he boasted, in a fine imitation of that perfectly nice young man with the sextant, Simon Harley-Dickinson.

Penelope suppressed a smile as she remembered her new acquaintance. What were the odds they might run into him again? London was an enormous city, of course, but for some reason she did not think they had seen the last of Simon.

And, although she felt a bit skittish about letting the *Hixby's* out of her sight (this was, as you no doubt recall, because of the regrettable incident on the train), she handed the guidebook over to Alexander with only the slightest hesitation.

"Very well, but mind you keep a close eye on it, Alexander. Now off we go, children. To the post office and then"—it gave her a thrilling feeling of butterflies in the tummy to even say the words—"Buckingham Palace!"

THE LONDON GENERAL POST OFFICE was so impressive that Penelope could hardly imagine how Buckingham Palace might surpass it—until they arrived at the palace, that is. Then she understood quite well, for there is a significant difference between a post office and a palace (and by this one should infer no disrespect to professional mail carriers, who serve an indispensable function in modern society and are much appreciated by all reasonable, letter-writing people).

"Look!" Cassiopeia pointed. "Home!"

"No, that is not Ashton Place," Penelope corrected, although Cassiopeia did have a point. Both Buckingham Palace and Ashton Place were fine examples of the neoclassical style of architecture, which is to say they were boxy and rather plain, in a symmetrical, fluted-column sort of way. But Buckingham Palace was inarguably grander, for it was a palace, after all, and the royal family actually lived there, at least when they were in town: Queen Victoria and Prince Albert and their many children, and, one presumes, the children's governess.

Penelope felt suddenly curious: Who was this royal governess? Where had she gone to school, and how did she go about her work? Educating children raised by wolves was one thing, but to be put in charge of actual princes and princesses? That was a job for a Swanburne girl if there ever was one. Somehow, though, Penelope doubted that any Poor Bright Female would be chosen for such an exalted position.

"But that is quite enough wondering about that," she told herself, for they had arrived at the gates of the palace, and it was no time to go off on a tangent. "Let us see what Mr. Hixby has to tell us about this architectural landmark," she said to the children, flipping through the guidebook. "I, for one, can never remember if those triangular bits above the columns are called pediments, or impediments—ah, here it is! Buckingham Palace. It says, 'The royal house is warm and fine, the cold and hungry wait in line.'"

"Poem," Beowulf observed.

"You are correct, Beowulf." Penelope shut the guidebook. She too had noticed that most of the entries were in the form of little poems, except for the one about Gallery Seventeen at the British Museum, which went on for pages. "How curious. I wonder what it means?"

"'Wait in line,' look." Alexander tugged at her sleeve and pointed.

Snaking all the way 'round the side of the palace and then back again was a long line of sad-faced, shabbily dressed people. There were old men and women, young ones, too, and many with small children huddled about their legs. They had an air of worry about them, as if a dark cloud of difficulty and disappointment was hanging low over their heads.

"Need a ticket?" The man's voice startled Penelope, and she found herself slipping the guidebook out of sight beneath her cloak. Alexander, Beowulf, and Cassiopeia each took a step closer to her.

"A ticket for what?" she asked.

"A ticket for the line." He was a small, wiry fellow in a long checkered coat. "Should've gotten here earlier if so. Today's tickets are long gone."

Cassiopeia peeked out from behind Penelope's skirts. "Tickawhy?"

The man lifted an eyebrow at Cassiopeia.

"She wants to know what all these people are waiting for," Penelope translated.

"Foreigners, huh?" He cast a sideways look at Cassiopeia, then clasped his hands in front of him and rolled his eyes heavenward. "Better days, miss! They're waiting for better days to come, and good luck to 'em, I say. Until then, a ticket'll get 'em a packet of leftover food from the palace kitchens." He rubbed his tummy and spoke slowly and loudly for the sake of the children. "They're waitin' for grub. It's the pauper's food line."

"That is generous, I suppose," Penelope replied

uncertainly. Leftovers to eat were surely better than nothing, but for a whole family to wait in line for scraps, like stray cats mewing at the kitchen door? It did not seem right to her.

"You don't need a ticket, then?" The man looked the children over with an appraising eye. Their hair was still a tangle (Penelope had been so eager to get them out of the house that she had not bothered to repair their attempts at combing), but their clothes were of decent quality and in good repair. "No offense, miss. Sorry to trouble you."

Penelope's eyes kept being drawn back to the hungry people in the line. She wondered how long they had been waiting. "I do not understand," she said to the man. "I thought you said today's tickets had all been disposed of?"

"Oh, they're gone, yes. Long gone. Still, for the right person and at the right price, a ticket can always be found." He turned over his hand and flashed what appeared to be an entire roll of tickets, which quickly disappeared into one of his many pockets.

Penelope could scarcely believe it. "Those tickets are meant to be charity for the poor; you said so yourself." She scolded. "I'm sure it is not right for you to take money for them. You ought to be ashamed—" But the man had already disappeared into the crowd, still searching for some poor soul desperate enough to pay for the free tickets he had somehow hoarded.

IN THE WORDS OF AGATHA Swanburne, "Don't look now, but everything's about to change." This incident was a perfect example of what the wise woman must have meant, for although Penelope had begun the day feeling positively chipper, she now found herself in a state that can only be described as high dudgeon.

"How infuriating!" she cried to no one in particular. "I am quite sure if Queen Victoria knew of this man's dishonesty, her majesty would be very unhappy indeed." And with that, Penelope started to march briskly toward the palace.

"Lumawoo!" the children called in alarm as they chased after her. "Where? Where?"

"I am going to request that a message be delivered to Queen Victoria," she explained, without breaking her stride.

"Victor*ahwoooooooooo*!" the children howled excitedly. Even as they scampered after their governess, the boys began practicing their bows and socially useful phrases: "Greetings, Your Majesty! How do you do? Lovely weather! The pleasure is mine," and so on, while Cassiopeia curtsied so low she toppled over and had to scurry to catch up.

"I doubt we shall get to meet her. The queen is very busy." Penelope's determination increased with each step. "But someone must tell her what is going on out here. Perhaps there is a constable who can help us." She looked around and saw a uniformed guard standing stiffly just outside the main gate. He was not a police officer, exactly, but he seemed to be in some official capacity; surely he would do just as well.

"Sir! Sir!" Penelope had reached the gate, and the children were close behind. "May I speak with you for a moment?"

The guard stood motionless. Not even his eyes moved.

"Pardon me, sir," Penelope repeated, rather forcefully, for a Swanburne girl in high dudgeon is nothing to trifle with. "There is a matter of some urgency which I would like brought to Her Majesty's attention at once. Can you help me?"

Unmoved by her plea, the guard stared straight ahead. For a moment Penelope wondered if he might be a statue. He cut a very dashing figure, to be sure, in a trim scarlet tunic over deep blue trousers, with a spotless white belt cinched about his waist. But the most striking thing about his uniform was the hat. It was enormous, for one thing, in the shape of a barrel, and it seemed to be made completely out of fur.

Now that Penelope was standing so close, she noticed how the mass of fur covered the top half of the guard's face in a way that made him seem not quite like a person at all. In fact, if not for the rest of the uniform, he might easily be mistaken for—

"Ahbear! Ahbear!"

"Ahwoooooooooooooooooooo!"

The children let loose a frenzy of howls. Beowulf paused long enough to take a deep sniff. "Ahbear!" he yelled conclusively, pointing at the guard's head. Cassiopeia curled into a tight crouch, ready to spring at the poor fellow. Alexander bared his teeth and emitted the most vicious growl imaginable.

"Ahbearrrrrrrrrrr!"

As one, they pounced.

"No! Children, stop! Do not attack!" Penelope was sick with fear. For the guard, being a guard, was armed with a musket. The weapon was now at his shoulder, and the muzzle was aimed straight at the Incorrigibles.

Without thinking about the consequences, Penelope, too, hurled herself at the guard.

"They are only children!" she cried. "Do not shoot!"

"Children? A pack of wolf cubs would be more like it." It was the guard speaking from someplace close by; for some reason Penelope could no longer see him, for she was suddenly in the dark. "Listen up, miss. It's my job to guard the queen's palace, and guard it I will. I'm on strict orders not to converse with the tourists, so you've already got me in trouble. Easy there, little fella! The hat's pure Canadian brown bear, and they cost a king's ransom. I'd hate to explain to my commanding officer why I need a new one."

Only then did Penelope realize that her eyes were squeezed shut in terror. Very slowly, she opened them, whereupon she beheld an astonishing sight: Cassiopeia had all four limbs wrapped around the guard's leg, with her teeth sunk into his trousers. Alexander dangled from the musket as if it were part of a jungle gym, while Beowulf was perched on the man's head, wrestling vigorously with the hat.

"Ahbear?" Cassiopeia asked curiously, gazing upward.

"It was a bear, once. Would you like to pet it?" The guard reached up and removed the hat, Beowulf and all, and held it out to the girl.

Alexander slid off the musket barrel and dropped to the ground. "Pardon me," he said, bowing to the

"They are only children!" she cried. *"Do not shoot!"*

guard. "How do you do?" Then both boys bowed, and Cassiopeia curtsied.

"The pleasure is mine, *woof*!" she said, in her piping voice. The guard was clearly impressed.

"That's very well said. I wish my boy had nice manners like you lot do." He turned to Penelope. "I can't help you with the queen, but if you have a suggestion, leave it in the suggestion box. That's the best I can do."

"Another time, perhaps. Thank you. I apologize for the disturbance." Penelope shepherded the three Incorrigibles away from the gate and across the plaza, until she spotted an empty park bench in a quiet spot. There she sat down, for her knees were shaking beneath her skirt, and she did not want the children to know.

The children, on the other hand, were now wonderfully energized. They argued about where go next.

"St. James's Park!"

"Big Ben!"

"The British Mew-eezum!" Cassiopeia suggested, adorably mispronouncing the word.

"Your enthusiasm is admirable, children." Penelope patted her forehead with a handkerchief. "But I must confess, I have had quite enough sightseeing for one day."

It was possible that a delayed-onset case of holiday

fatigue was finally catching up with the usually plucky young governess. Or perhaps the sight of the three Incorrigible children once again facing down the barrel of a musket (just as they had on the fateful day when Lord Fredrick Ashton discovered them running wild in the woods of Ashton Place, and was prevented from shooting only by the quick intervention of Old Timothy, the enigmatic coachman)—well, it was simply too much for Penelope to bear, if one will pardon the expression.

The children were clearly disappointed. But their governess had made up her mind, and that, they knew very well, was that. In any case, it had been a good while since breakfast, and all four of them were in need of tea and something sweet to nibble on.

So, without further discussion, and with Alexander still in charge of the *Hixby's Guide*, Penelope and the Incorrigible children headed home. No doubt it was the holiday fatigue at work, but Penelope could scarcely bring herself to sightsee as they walked. She had expected London to be a glittering metropolis full of culture and learning. Instead, it seemed like the forest of Ashton Place—an Ominous Landscape full of danger at every turn.

It was not until her thoughts had strayed to Ashton

Place in this unexpected fashion, and Alexander had successfully navigated them back to Number Twelve Muffinshire Lane, that Penelope realized: In all the excitement, they had completely forgotten to buy a postcard for Nutsawoo.

THE SIXTH CHAPTER

Penelope finds a new
creature to tame.

AFTER SUCH AN EVENTFUL MORNING, Penelope was in need of peaceful, calming pursuits. She looked forward to a bit of poetry read aloud, some quiet work on the children's journals, and possibly a nap, if the Incorrigibles could be persuaded.

But she and the children returned to find Number Twelve Muffinshire Lane in an uproar. The servants from Ashton Place were frantically cleaning the already spotless house: airing out linens, dusting bric-a-brac, making up beds, sweeping the carpets, polishing woodwork, and otherwise getting things spick-and-span for the imminent appearance of Lady Constance and Lord Fredrick.

The hubbub was at such a fever pitch that even Mrs. Clarke could not hold still long enough to say a proper good morning to Penelope and the children, though she had scarcely seen them since their arrival in London.

"Ahhhhhhh!" Mrs. Clarke cried as she propelled herself from one task to the next. The way she kept moving as she spoke gave her voice an oddly sirenlike quality, as it got LOUDER and softer and LOUDER and softer, depending on whether she was coming or going. "Miss Lumley, wherever have you been? I thought you and the children must have fallen in the Thames! Well, don't just stand there blocking traffic—whoops! Restrain yourself, Margaret! If you use that much polish on the floor we'll have to wear ice skates to shimmy ourselves from room to room."

If Penelope had been in a jollier mood, the idea of Mrs. Clarke in a pair of ice skates, gracefully twirling and leaping across a frozen expanse, would have made her struggle not to laugh. As it was, she merely said, "Mrs. Clarke, the children and I are in urgent need of some tea. May we fix it ourselves in the kitchen and bring it upstairs? We will be sure to stay out of your way."

"Fix it yourselves? Bring it upstairs? I should say not! We can't afford any spills. I'll have Margaret carry it up, before she polishes a hole in the floor. And mind you don't leave any fingerprints on the banister," Mrs. Clarke called over her shoulder (for she was now whizzing into the dining room). "Lord and Lady Ashton will be here before dinner—how's that silver coming along, Suzy?—and everything has to be just so."

Already she was on her way back; truly, ice skates would have been a time-saver. "Missed a spot on the ladle, Sue! Oh, Miss Lumley, before I forget, a letter came for you. It's on the tray table by the stair—careful, Gladys! That's a feather duster, not a cricket bat! Be gentle with the potted plant, or soon it won't have a leaf to call its own."

"Frond," Alexander corrected, for the plant in question was, in fact, a fern, and thus its leaves were properly called fronds. Ordinarily Penelope would have been very proud of his pteridomaniacal expertise, but at the word "letter" her mind had skipped off on a tangent from which it had not yet returned.

"Not only is the General Post Office a handsome building, it is a model of brisk efficiency as well," she thought. "For I only just mailed my letter to Miss Mortimer this morning, and look: The reply has already come." The very idea of such prompt, no-nonsense execution of one's responsibilities was so admirably Swanburne-like that Penelope's spirits were quite lifted.

As well they should be, for in Miss Penelope Lumley's day the London post office was nothing if not efficient. Deliveries were made five times daily, thanks to a fleet-footed army of postal workers who whisked the mail from here to there before one could say jackrabbit. Affixed with a one-cent stamp bearing the likeness of Queen Victoria herself, a letter would reach its destination within hours of the time it was sent.

Penelope was so dazzled by this marvelous display of postal competence—and for a mere penny, mind you, as long as the letter weighed less than half on ounce—she did not even notice that the correspondence in her hand was not from Miss Mortimer at all. Only after she had made her way upstairs, set the children to work on their journals, added two sugars and a splash of cream to her tea, and given it a stir (to her credit, Margaret had delivered the tea tray without spilling a single drop, and managed a small plate of biscuits, too)—only then did Penelope settle herself in a chair, slit open the envelope, and begin to read.

Dear Miss Lumley,

    Well, it was a treat to meet you and the children. Wanted to tell you I've begun work on several new plays at once; thanks for all the inspiration!

    Just a reminder: If you keep the North Star in view, and the wind at your back, you'll have no problem at all navigating wherever you please.

Cheers,

SHD

"Why, this is from Simon Harley-Dickinson!" she exclaimed. Then she clapped her hand over her mouth, for even she did not fully understand why she would be made so excited by the receipt of this brief correspondence from the wrong person.

"Lumawoo happy," Beowulf observed as he dabbed at his watercolors.

"New friend," Alexander agreed, pausing to sharpen a pencil.

"Simawoo," Cassiopeia chanted absently as she drew. "Simawoo, Simawoo, Sim*ahwooooooo—*"

"Tut-tut, children! That is enough conversation for now; please attend to your journals." Penelope tucked the letter into her apron pocket and quickly regained her professional composure, on the outside, at least.

For a few minutes, the scratching of pens and swirling of paintbrushes were the only sounds in the tiny, makeshift nursery. Then:

"As Agatha Swanawoo say: Less talk, more do." Alexander sounded completely serious, and he and his siblings had their heads bent over their work, but it seemed to Penelope that all three of the Incorrigibles were suppressing giggles. She put on her sternest governess voice.

"No doubt Agatha Swanburne did say something along those lines, but whether she did or not, it is advice well worth taking. Now, how are your journal entries about our trip to Buckingham Palace coming along? Do you have any questions about neoclassical architecture? The use of pediments? The practice of primogeniture in the British hereditary monarchy?" Penelope knew she was babbling, but she could not help it. The unexpected letter from Simon seemed to have made her brain go all fizzy.

"Done." Alexander put down his pencil and proudly held out the paper to Penelope. At a much larger scale, Alexander had sketched his own childlike version of the type of alpine scenery depicted in the tiny watercolors of the *Hixby's Guide*. His landscape featured a crystal blue lake and a meadow dotted with pretty white flowers, with snowcapped peaks in the distance.

The drawing took Penelope by surprise, but she could hardly say she was disappointed, for it was a very charming picture. "Alexander, how delightful!" she said warmly. "When I look at this, I feel as if I can smell the fresh mountain air." She demonstrated by sniffing. "See? It is so vivid as to seem almost like a familiar place to me. Let us put it somewhere safe to dry."

Pleased, Alexander spread the picture on a windowsill and weighed the corners down with books so it would not blow away.

"Cassawoof done, too." Cassiopeia waved her page around, eager to hear her teacher's praise. Penelope took hold of the drawing with a smile that quickly faded, for the child had filled the page with a tall, menacing scribble of brown. It had a white stripe across its middle and what looked like a red shirt above.

The figure held up its arms in a most threatening way. Worse, it possessed long, sharp claws that dripped with streaks of red—was it supposed to be blood?

"Ahbear," Cassiopeia explained proudly. Then she held out her arms and stiffened her fingers, just like the claws in the picture. "Grrrrrrrr!" she growled, showing her teeth. She lurched toward her elder brother with bear arms outstretched.

Alexander, playing along, lifted his arm as if it were a musket—

"Yes, yes, I understand," Penelope interrupted, as she anxiously pressed Alexander's arm down and away. "You have drawn a bear, but you are also thinking of the guard's uniform, so the bear is wearing clothes. But it is still a bear, and a frightening one, too."

"Ahbear," Cassiopeia agreed. Playfully she added one last, bloodthirsty growl: *"Ahbearrrrrrrr!"*

"Such convincing bear noises, Cassiopeia! If you are not careful, you may well end up on the stage yourself. Now, let us see what Beowulf has done." Penelope was determined to change the subject away from evil bears and dangerous muskets. And she knew Beowulf was quite talented at drawing; by now he had no doubt sketched a scale diagram of Buckingham Palace's fluted columns and soothing symmetrical features, with no bloody claws to be seen. At least, that is what Penelope hoped.

"Not finished," he said humbly, then shrugged and held out the page.

Beowulf's picture was far more elaborate than those of his siblings, and it did need a bit more work coloring in the background, but the gist of it was on full, frightening view.

In the sky: a full moon, its eerie glow partially obscured by dark, swirling clouds.

In the foreground: the dense, ferny undergrowth of a forest, bordered by a few gnarled tree trunks rising upward.

In the center of the page: an old woman, wrapped in a cloak. Her mouth hung open in a leering smile, and her teeth were large and razor sharp, with a prominent set of gleaming white incisors. From the back of her shroudlike garments poked a long, wolfish tail.

Cassiopeia and Alexander clapped and barked with admiration, but Penelope's skin went cold. "Is that the Gypsy woman we met yesterday?" she asked, already knowing it must be. The likeness was remarkable, except, of course, for the teeth and tail.

Beowulf nodded. "The hunt is on," he said tremulously. At the remark, both of his siblings sank into defensive crouches and began to whimper.

"Why, Beowulf, whatever do you mean?" Penelope asked, looking with alarm at her three suddenly anxious pupils.

The children did not answer, at least, not directly. *"Ahwooooooo,"* they began to cry softly. *"Ahwooooo, ahwooooo!"*

The howls quickly gained in volume, which

prompted Penelope to jump up and close the windows. Although she had little experience of city life, she was quite sure that three children baying and barking at full throttle would not be a welcome addition to the neighborhood.

Returning to her chair, she drew the Incorrigibles close to her and tried her best to sound reassuring. "What a marvelous imagination you have, Beowulf, to have invented a scene so dramatic and frightening! Of course, the Gypsy woman was real enough," she went on. "But the teeth, and tail, and that ominous moon— these are only make-believe, so there is no need to be upset."

The children did not look convinced. Penelope was about to explain how a journal is a true record of events, and not a collection of alarming fantasies about sharp-toothed Gypsies with bristly tails—but something in the children's faces made her stop and ask, "Wait . . . did something unpleasant happen when I left you alone with that strange woman?"

"The hunt is on!" the Incorrigibles cried, followed by many urgent howls of *"Ahwooooooooooo! Ahwooooooooooo!"*

Penelope stroked the children's heads and murmured soothing noises. "'The hunt is on.' What a thing for her to say! I should like to ask her what she meant by it," she thought determinedly. "Perhaps Mr. Harley-Dickinson knows who she is, and how she can be reached; after all, she did frequent his neighborhood. I will write to him at once."

When the carriage from Ashton Place finally pulled up to the entrance of Number Twelve Muffinshire Lane, and Old Timothy, the coachman, held open the door, only Lady Constance emerged.

Penelope watched from one of the windows upstairs. Was Old Timothy friend or foe? She still suspected that he might have been the culprit who released the squirrel at the holiday ball, in order to provoke the children into wolfish fits. And yet, if not for Old Timothy, the three Incorrigibles would never have been rescued from the forest of Ashton Place to begin with. Instead, they might have ended up in the same predicament as the many hunting trophies in Lord Fredrick's study, with their shining glass eyes and stiff, taxidermic poses—oh, it was too awful to think about!

The servants streamed out from the house like ants to remove Lady Constance's many floral-upholstered trunks from the carriage. The children had worn themselves out with howling and were now quietly practicing their cursive letters, so Penelope opened the windows again and listened. Lady Constance's voice carried clearly from the cobblestone street below.

"Lord Fredrick will be here in time for supper. He has many acquaintances in the city, and wished to pay a call at his club's accommodations in London before settling in. It is quite understandable." Lady Constance sounded merry in the sort of brightly exaggerated way that made it clear she was trying not to cry, and perhaps not entirely succeeding.

"Poor Lady Constance," Penelope thought, with a rush of sympathy. "Lord Fredrick pays scarcely any attention to her at all. Perhaps that is why she is so ill-tempered so much of the time."

This may seem an astute observation for a fifteen-year-old girl with no personal experience of marriage to make (as previously mentioned, Penelope had had scarce contact with boys in general, never mind prospective husbands). But she had long ago learned from Dr. Westminster, the Swanburne veterinarian, that some creatures become perfectly miserable when left alone too much, and this misery can easily turn to viciousness. As a result, their caretakers and fellow creatures give them a wide berth, which only makes them more lonely, mistrustful, and snappish than before.

A great deal of kindness and patience (not to mention quick reflexes and an ample supply of treats) are required to turn a situation like this around without getting badly bitten. Could such a cure be achieved with Lady Constance?

If so, Penelope theorized, and if Lady Constance were not so terribly spoiled but had instead had the benefit of a more Swanburne-like education, she might well turn out to be a perfectly pleasant companion. She and Penelope might even be friends, were it not for the vast difference in their social stations, what with Lady Constance being a lady and Penelope being a lowly governess.

"Dear me, that is a lot of 'ifs' and 'might have beens,'" Penelope concluded. "But still, there is no harm in offering a friendly greeting. Today she will be tired from her long journey, but perhaps tomorrow, after I have done with the children's lessons for the day, I will go downstairs on some pretext or other and see if I can engage Lady Constance in pleasant conversation. It would be the kind and generous thing—the Swanburne thing—to do."

THE SEVENTH CHAPTER

*Lady Constance endures a series
of postal disappointments.*

A WELL-KNOWN POET—not Henry Wadsworth Long-fellow, who wrote "The Wreck of the Hesperus," a poem with which the Incorrigible children were already quite familiar, but a different poet, named Robert Burns—once wrote a poem called, simply, "To a Mouse."

Now, you might find this title silly and even a bit misleading, for what famous poet writes poems to mice? Especially when there are so many shipwrecks, headless horsemen, gloomy talking birds, and other equally fascinating topics to write poems about?

On the other hand, perhaps Mr. Burns was using his poetic license. This is the license that allows poets to say things that are not precisely true without being accused of telling lies. Anyone may obtain such a license, but still, the powers it grants must be wielded responsibly. (A word to the wise: When asked, "Who put the empty milk carton back in the refrigerator?" if you reply, "My incorrigible sister, Lavinia," when in fact it is you who are the guilty party, at the ensuing trial, the judge will not be impressed to hear you defend yourself by claiming that your whopper was merely "poetic license.")

However, the title "To a Mouse" is not an example of poetic license, for the poem was, in fact, written to a mouse, which simply goes to prove that one never knows from what furry little rodent inspiration will strike. In Mr. Burns's case, inspiration struck the poet soon after his plow struck the nest of a "wee beastie," which is to say, a small field mouse, and tore it all to pieces. His eight-stanza apology includes the memorable lines:

The best-laid schemes o' mice an' men
Gang aft agley . . .

It should be pointed out that the poem is written in an old Scottish dialect, and thus contains words that are rarely used nowadays, even in Scotland. To "gang aft agley" means to "often go astray." What Mr. Burns was driving at was this: The mouse, who had built herself a cozy nest and was no doubt feeling quite smug about it, was now flat out of luck, and that is simply the way life goes, not only for mice but for people, too. One thing is planned, and yet something quite different actually occurs. A careless poet accidentally plows your mouse house to bits, an important appointment is missed due to a flat tire on one's velocipede, or a well-intended and perfectly friendly overture is interpreted as something else altogether.

Thus it was the next day, when Penelope eventually went downstairs to strike up a conversation with Lady Constance. Her impulse to offer some fellowship was a kind and noble one, and yet it was received in an entirely different spirit—for one of the disadvantages of having a postal delivery five times daily is that it creates so many opportunities to be disappointed when a much-longed-for invitation fails, and fails, and fails yet again, to arrive.

The morning post had brought nothing to the house but the day's newspaper. The midday post had brought an advertisement promoting the skills of a local chimney sweep. Now it was nearly three o'clock, and another post was due any moment. It was Margaret's duty to await the postman by the front door, silver letter tray in hand.

As was always the case at mail time, there were two sharp raps on the knocker, after which the mail came sliding through a brass mail slot in the lower part of the heavy wooden door.

Knock! Knock!

"Is it the post?" Lady Constance's voice rang eagerly down the stairs.

"Yes, my lady, but—"

"The post! The post!" Lady Constance clattered down two flights at a dangerous pace. She ran so fast her hair came undone and popped up in yellow curlicues all 'round her head. "The afternoon post, at last! For this morning I sent word to all my acquaintances in town saying that I had arrived. I expect to be *buried* in luncheon invitations, and dinner parties, too, of course, and asked on all manner of excursions—Margaret, remind me to tell Mrs. Clarke: We ought to offer a small gratuity to the postman; his mailbag is bound to be extra heavy for the duration of our stay in London—"

But there was nothing on Margaret's tray except a brochure for Dr. Phelps's Miracle Cream: "Guaranteed to Remove Wrinkles, Spots, Warts, and Lumps!"

The drama would be played out again at five o'clock, and finally at eight. By that point Lady Constance was in a foul mood; the lack of correspondence seemed to be taking a dreadful toll on her already delicate constitution. She refused her supper and instead demanded a particular type of marzipan that Mrs. Clarke had to send the young houseboy, Jasper, scurrying all over London to find. Then she very nearly scalded herself in the newfangled bathtub, and had to be lifted out red faced and yelling by two terrified ladies' maids.

Lord Fredrick had scarcely been home at all ("Business, dear," he had explained as he rushed out the door right after breakfast). In short, Lady Constance was on her very last nerve, and the final post of the day was due in exactly one and one-half minutes.

Alas, it was at this very moment, after the Incorrigibles had been tucked into their beds, that Penelope came downstairs. The intention to show a bit of warmth to her mistress was still firmly lodged in her mind. She knew nothing about Lady Constance's postal disappointments, since she herself had been happily occupied all day, strolling the parks of London while studying latitude and longitude with the children. This was at Alexander's request; he was quite taken with the topic of navigation all of a sudden and refused to go ten steps in any direction without referring to his compass. And the children had showed admirable restraint when it came to both squirrels and pigeons; Penelope had only had to offer a few cautionary reminders and the occasional distracting biscuit.

Yes, Penelope was in quite a different mood than poor Lady Constance, for the very notion of navigation made her think of Simon, and the thought of Simon made her giddy—giddy enough to be idly whistling the same lilting sea chantey that Simon himself was prone to whistle when taking a reading on his sextant, as she skipped lightly down the stairs. And Penelope, too, was half expecting a letter, for she had written to Simon in that morning's post inquiring about the Gypsy woman. Might a reply be on its way already? Clearly, in London, anything was possible.

"Good evening, Lady Constance," she called out cheerfully when she spotted the lady standing next to Margaret at the front door. "Welcome to Muffinshire Lane! Isn't London marvelous?"

Lady Constance turned, and Penelope saw that her usually perfectly dressed and coiffed mistress was, to be kind, a wreck: Her cheeks were scalded, her hair was frizzed, and her eyes were puffy and ringed 'round with dark, exhausted circles, like those of a raccoon.

"I fail to see what is so marvelous, Miss Lumley," she snapped. Then she spun back to Margaret and began desperately wringing her hands.

"This is the last post of the day, is it not?"

"Yes, my lady, but—"

"Why is it so *late*?"

Margaret swallowed anxiously. "It has not yet struck eight o'clock, my lady. I am sure he will be here soon—"

Knock! Knock!

There were the two raps on the door. Penelope watched, puzzled, as Lady Constance gasped and clutched at her throat. Margaret stood in readiness as a single, elegant envelope poked through the slot and dropped noiselessly on the tray.

"Finally!" Lady Constance shrieked. "Is that it? There is only the one?"

"Yes, my lady, but—"

"Let me have it, please."

"Yes, my lady, but—"

Terror had reduced Margaret to a single phrase, yet no matter how many times she uttered it, Lady Constance paid her no mind.

"Let me have it right now, or I will take it myself!"

Lady Constance hurled herself forward to snatch the letter.

"But—it's for Miss Lumley, m'lady," Margaret squeaked. She curtsied low, and extended the tray to Penelope.

The grim silence as Penelope gingerly descended the bottom step, walked five paces forward, and took the lovely cream-colored envelope from Margaret's tray was broken only by the *cuckoo-cuckoo-cuckoo* of a grandfather clock in the hall, striking the hour. That meant Lady Constance had eight full *cuckoos* to build up a head of steam. She used the time well, and when the eighth cuckoo was done, she let loose.

"Miss Lumley, do my eyes deceive me? This is the most impertinent thing I have ever heard of!"

"Perhaps it's from the same gentleman who wrote to you yesterday," Margaret squeaked in a confidential tone. Alas, it was not confidential enough. Lady Constance took a menacing step toward Penelope.

"Yesterday? Do you mean to tell me that you—a mere governess!—have received *two* separate pieces of correspondence since arriving in London, while I have received *none whatsoever*?"

"I do apologize, Lady Constance." Penelope keenly wanted to glance at the envelope to see if it was, in fact, from Simon, but she dared not in front of Lady Constance, who looked as if she might tear it to shreds with her teeth. "It was not my intention to receive any letters. They simply . . . arrived."

And then, perhaps unwisely, she added, "Do you know that poem by Mr. Robert Burns, called 'To a Mouse'? I was just reading it to the children before bedtime. It makes rather the same point, about things not happening in the way we expect. 'The best-laid plans of mice and men—'"

But, much as she would have liked to, Penelope did not get to pronounce "gang aft agley," because Lady Constance was not listening. "Humph!" Lady Constance said, speechless with fury. She said it again. "Humph!" Then she stormed back upstairs to her lavishly decorated but friendless suite of rooms, leaving Penelope and Margaret staring at their shoes, at least until Lady Constance was well out of sight.

Then, without risking any animated conversation, exclamations of delight, or other audible signs of happiness that might provoke their mistress further, Margaret simply handed Penelope the silver letter opener, which had been lying unused all day on the tray. Her expression of intense, agonizing curiosity said the rest, as did the excited way she pranced in place and the soundless giggles that she carefully muffled with her free hand.

But the letter was not from Simon at all. It was a reply from Miss Charlotte Mortimer! Once she realized that, Penelope was even happier than she had been before, though it was a different sort of happy.

Happy, that is, until she read the letter.

My dear Penny,

I am so relieved to hear that you and the children made it to London without incident. Did the Hixby's Guide *lead the way?*

Please join me for luncheon tomorrow, in the Fern Court at the Piazza Hotel. Though I long to meet your three pupils, and plan to do so at the earliest safe opportunity, for now it is best that we talk alone. I have news, not all of it good, and none of it for children's ears.

I ask that you keep the time and place of our meeting to yourself. I shall be there at twelve sharp; look for me by the Osmunda regalis.

Do be careful.

> *Yours as ever,*
> *Miss Charlotte Mortimer*

THE EIGHTH CHAPTER

*At long last: Penelope is reunited
with Miss Charlotte Mortimer.*

GIVEN THAT FERNS ARE NOT nearly as popular as they once were, you can hardly be expected to know that *Osmunda regalis* is the scientific name of the much-admired royal fern. It is a truly spectacular variety that can easily grow six feet tall, with arching, attractively shaped fronds and spore-bearing stalks that turn a pleasing shade of brown when fully mature.

The spore-bearing stalks are called "sporangia." Many would no doubt argue that "sporangia" is hardly a word worth memorizing, yet one never knows when ferns will make a comeback. The forward-thinking among you would do well to jot it down.

Sadly, the Piazza Hotel has long since been demolished to make way for the sorts of retail establishments that people seem to prefer nowadays: boutiques selling new clothes that have been made to look worn, banks that have run out of money, and cafés that brew coffee so strong as to be virtually undrinkable. But on the long-ago day that Miss Penelope Lumley was scheduled to dine with Miss Charlotte Mortimer, the Fern Court at the Piazza Hotel was in its prime. Its magnificent display of potted ferns was famous throughout Europe, as was its mouthwatering and inventive cuisine, courtesy of the legendary Chef Philippe, a true master of the cutting board.

Under normal circumstances, Penelope would have been surprised that the usually no-frills Miss Mortimer had chosen such an elegant restaurant for their meeting. She would have been thrilled at the prospect of seeing an important collection of ferns, and even felt some anticipatory tummy rumbles at the thought of eating what promised to be a truly delicious meal.

However, just as a carelessly spilled puddle of India ink blots out the line of practice cursive letters painstakingly written on the paper beneath, the anxiety-producing contents of Miss Mortimer's letter blotted out any other emotions Penelope may have had. What did Miss Mortimer mean, that it was not "safe" to bring the children? And that she had bad news to deliver? And that Penelope should tell no one about their meeting?

A chance encounter with a pickpocket on a train, a greedy scoundrel in front of Buckingham Palace, a strange remark from a fortune-teller, a mistress in high dudgeon—these were life's minor annoyances, and Penelope knew better than to make too much of them. But Miss Mortimer's letter seemed to imply that there was actual trouble afoot. What on earth could it be?

All these worries and more swirled through Penelope's mind as she dressed for this long-awaited reunion. She briefly considered putting on the fine gray dress that she had worn to the Ashton Place holiday ball, but just thinking about the disastrous consequences of that night made her slip on one of her usual brown woolen frocks instead.

She took deep breaths to calm herself, as all the girls at Swanburne were taught to do in a class called Do Not Panic: A Swanburne Girl Always Keeps Her Wits About Her. After a few inhales through the nose and exhales through the mouth, Penelope felt that her wits were, if not directly about her, at least within arm's reach.

"Since I have never eaten in a fancy restaurant before, the experience is bound to be educational," she thought, with a renewed sense of purpose. "In any case, the only way to find out what Miss Mortimer has to say is to go and hear it for myself. Dear Miss Mortimer! I hope she is not too changed, after all these months."

And so, with her eagerness to see her former headmistress only slightly dimmed by worry, and after obtaining assurances from Margaret that she would keep a close eye on the children while Penelope was out (since Penelope was forbidden to tell where she was going, her evasive reply that she would be "having lunch with a friend" simply made Margaret giggle and squeal about Simon Harley-Dickinson all the more), Penelope double-checked the map, put on her best hat—which is to say, her only hat—and set off for the Piazza Hotel.

"Your table is this way, Miss Regalis."

Try as she might, Penelope had not been able to make the maître d' at the Fern Court understand that the reservation was not under the *name* Osmunda

Regalis, but that she was intending to meet someone *near* the *Osmunda regalis*. Still, she knew he was leading her in the right direction, for even among so many magnificent varieties the *regalis* were impossible to miss. The many potted specimens created a jungled grotto on the far side of the dining room, and the diners within, if any, were well concealed by the delicately swaying fronds.

Penelope wondered if it was a desire for secrecy that had prompted Miss Mortimer's choice of restaurant, and not just an appreciation for ferns—but she did not have to wonder for long. With a flourish, the maître d' held back an armful of foliage so that Penelope could enter the leafy, secluded room. There, at a charming table for two, with her only companion being the thin plume of steam that rose lazily from the teapot before her, sat Miss Charlotte Mortimer.

Changed or unchanged, bad news or good, it no longer mattered. The mere sight of her former headmistress, with her long, dark blond hair pulled back in its familiar pretty chignon at the base of her neck and her graceful, perfectly upright posture on display even as she sat reading the newspaper (as Agatha Swanburne once said, "To be kept waiting is unfortunate, but to be kept waiting with nothing interesting to read is a tragedy of Greek proportions")—why, it was all Penelope could do not to break into a run and hurl herself into Miss Mortimer's lap, just as she used to do as a child.

"But she is no longer my headmistress; now we are colleagues and friends," she reminded herself. "I must restrain myself from acting like a schoolgirl, for those days are behind me." And with that, she smiled, extended her hand, and spoke. "Miss Mortimer! How nice it is to see you!"

"Penny, dear Penny!" Ignoring Penelope's offer of a handshake, Miss Mortimer flew to her feet and hugged her former student tightly. When she finally pulled away, her eyes glistened.

"It is wonderful to see you, too, my dear. It has been much, much too long. But you are always in my thoughts, believe me." Her smile was so tender, and the feeling in her voice was so warm and genuine, that Penelope felt all her newfound professionalism melt into a puddle. How silly she had been to think that time, distance, or anything else would ever alter her friendship with Miss Mortimer!

The kind headmistress gestured for Penelope to sit. "I hope you do not mind; I have already ordered lunch for us both. The food here is just as good as people say, but you absolutely must save room for dessert—dear me, Penny! How grown-up you look! You have become quite pretty, did you know that?"

This unexpected compliment threw Penelope for a loop. "Oh—oh, my!" she stammered. "Really, Miss Mortimer . . . I hardly think so . . . the light here among the ferns must be rather dim. . . ."

"I assure you, I can see perfectly well. Even your hair has changed. . . ." Miss Mortimer frowned. "I think you have not been using the Swanburne hair poultice, as I asked you to do; am I right? Well, we shall discuss that shortly." She unfolded her crisp white napkin and placed it neatly across her lap. "Forgive me for asking, Penny, but I must know: While you are here with me, are the children being attended to?"

"Of course." Penelope carefully imitated Miss Mortimer's actions regarding the napkin. "There is a young housemaid named Margaret, one of the staff from Ashton Place who has accompanied the family to London. She is watching them during my absence."

"I see. And this Margaret—is she trustworthy?"

"She is young, and can be silly at times." Penelope remembered the giddy way Margaret had teased her about Simon. "I suspect she may not be a very good housemaid; Mrs. Clarke is always scolding her about this and that. But when it comes to the well-being of the children: Yes, she is completely trustworthy."

"I am glad to hear it." Miss Mortimer's serious expression softened. "Patient Penelope! I know you must be full of questions, and yet you sit there so calmly, as if nothing I might tell you could rattle your confidence. I admire your courage more than I can say. You do the Swanburne Academy proud."

Penelope murmured humble thanks, but inside she was beaming—and increasingly curious.

"In my letter, I said I had some news for you. But first I must hear about the children." Miss Mortimer leaned forward and lowered her voice, though they were the only diners in this hidden grotto. "Do they ever speak of their days in the forest? Does Alexander, in particular, remember anything of a time that may have come before?"

"They have not mentioned anything to me about it." Penelope spoke in a similarly hushed tone, since it would have felt awkward to answer in any other manner. "But it is obvious from the way they behave that they spent their time in the company of wild animals. Despite their academic accomplishments, they remain very fond of howling and are prone to chasing small, edible creatures. And Beowulf does

112

tend to chew. Especially shoes."

"How fascinating." Miss Mortimer sat back and sipped her tea. "Tell me more."

"They can be provoked by other things as well." Like any proud teacher Penelope loved nothing more than to talk about her students. "Why, just the other day, our trip to Buckingham Palace was cut short when the children mistook one of the palace guards for a bear. It caused quite a commotion."

Miss Mortimer began to laugh. "A bear!" she exclaimed. "Why? Because of the hat? Oh, that is priceless!"

Miss Mortimer's unexpected reaction jolted Penelope into a useful change of perspective: That terrifying business with the guard was nothing more than a funny escapade, really! Why had she not seen it that way before?

"Yes, it was quite a comedy," she said, laughing along with Miss Mortimer. "Beowulf actually climbed on top of the guard's head!"

"His head? Oh, my!"

Now the two of them were so merry that Penelope could barely finish the story; she was too busy gasping for air. "And Cassiopeia . . . tried to bite . . . his leg!"

"Ha ha ha ha!" Miss Mortimer had to wipe tears of mirth from the corner of her eye with the napkin.

"We had another hilarious mix-up, too, with a Gypsy fortune-teller!" Penelope went on in the same jovial spirit, for if one unpleasant episode could be made into an amusing anecdote, why not all of them? "Oh, the children were distraught! They howled up a storm, and later kept repeating some odd words the woman said to them: 'The hunt is on.' Ha ha ha ha!"

It took Penelope a few seconds to realize that Miss Mortimer had stopped laughing. Not only that. The expression on her face had altered in a way that made Penelope feel chilled to the bone.

"'The hunt is on?'" Miss Mortimer whispered. Her eyes darted around, as if she were worried someone might be eavesdropping. "Are you sure that is what she said?"

"That is what the children told me." Now all of Penelope's worry came rushing back at once, like a tidal wave, and the questions poured out: "Miss Mortimer, why does that disturb you so? Why was it not safe for the children to come to lunch? What is the bad news you have for me?"

Miss Mortimer opened her mouth to reply, but at that very moment the most mouthwatering aroma Penelope had ever smelled in her life wafted over to their table.

It was their first course, being wheeled through the ferns on a cart. Penelope and Miss Mortimer sat in awestruck silence as the waiter uncovered their appetizer plates. Penelope could not tell what it was. But the smell! It was positively scrumptious.

Miss Mortimer inhaled appreciatively, picked up her fork, and took a slow, savoring bite. "Fiddleheads Philippe," she said. "Try it. You will be amazed."

"Fiddleheads?"

"Ferns," Miss Mortimer explained. "The curly tips of unfurled fern fronds. It makes an excellent tongue twister, doesn't it? Unfurled fern fronds! Unfurled fern fronds!"

Only after Penelope had mastered saying "unfurled fern fronds," tasted the fiddleheads Philippe, and admitted that they were beyond her wildest imaginings of deliciousness, did Miss Mortimer begin to answer her questions.

"The hunt is on," she repeated, shaking her head. "It is remarkable that you should have been given such a warning, but nothing surprises me anymore. Penelope, the bad news is simply this: The children are in danger, even more so now than when they lived in the forest."

"What kind of danger?" Penelope exclaimed. "Why? From what source?"

Miss Mortimer paused and stared at her plate for a moment, as if some other, happier pronouncement might yet reveal itself there. "There is someone who wishes them ill, but he will not—he cannot—harm them directly. However, he will do whatever he can to put them in danger's path. You have already seen evidence of this."

"You mean, at the holiday ball?"

The headmistress nodded. "When I received your letter some months ago, telling me of the strange events of that evening, my suspicions were aroused. After much reflection I thought I would share my concerns with you. I wanted to do it in person; it is why I asked you to come to London. But this warning from the fortune-teller confirms it. Penelope, do you believe in the supernatural?"

Penelope took another bite, for no conversation, however disturbing, could ruin a dish this tasty. "Certainly not. But I did hear Lady Constance say once that Ashton Place must be cursed."

Miss Mortimer was so startled she almost dropped her fork. "She was complaining about how long the repairs were taking," Penelope quickly explained. "It

"Penelope, do you believe in the supernatural?"

was only a metaphor, I am sure! But why do you ask? Surely you do not put any stock in curses and crystal balls and such, do you?"

"There was a time I did not." Miss Mortimer looked uneasy. "But as Agatha Swanburne once said, 'An open mind—'"

"'Lets ideas out, as well as in.' I know." Penelope's thoughts began picking up speed all on their own, like a ball rolling downhill. "Do you mean to suggest that there *is* some curse on Ashton Place? Or that the Gypsy might know something about the person who wishes ill to the children? For I have already sent an inquiry to a recent acquaintance, whom I hope can arrange an interview with the old woman. Never fear, Miss Mortimer! I am determined to get to the bottom of it all."

"No!" Even though Miss Mortimer kept her voice low, there was no missing her sharp tone. "Penelope, you must obey me in this. Do not go around asking questions. When I invited you to lunch, I had resolved to give you a general instruction to be on your guard; I felt it was prudent. I did not want the children here because I did not want them to be frightened. But your news about the fortune-teller's warning took me by surprise, and I have already revealed more than I should."

She looked at Penelope intently. "About curses and prophecies I will say nothing more. But you must take this to heart: It is in your best interest, and that of the children, that you not seek to know any more about this unfortunate business than you do right now."

"But . . . 'A Swanburne girl is curious!' 'A Swanburne girl asks questions!'" Penelope protested, reciting the very maxims her headmistress and the other teachers at Swanburne had instilled in her.

Miss Mortimer smiled. "Believe me when I say: On this particular point, no one would agree with me more than Agatha Swanburne herself."

"But how am I to protect the children if I do not know what kind of danger they are in, or from what source?"

Miss Mortimer took another bite and gestured for Penelope to do the same. "The same way you have protected them so far. By having faith in them and seeing the best in them, and teaching them to see the best in themselves. Why, if you had not shown such compassion and love to the Incorrigible children, how would they have ever been able to make a friend of Nutsawoo?"

"Nutsawoo?" Now Penelope felt hopelessly

confused. "What does that silly little squirrel have to do with any of this?"

"'No one's fate is written in India ink,' as Agatha Swanburne once said." Miss Mortimer underscored the point by gesturing with her fork. "The hunt is on, indeed. But the hunt can end in unexpected ways. The Incorrigibles and Nutsawoo have already taught us that much. Do you understand?"

Penelope thought back to the night of the holiday ball, and the mad chase Nutsawoo had led through the house, with the children in pursuit. She remembered how desperately she had tried to find them, and how convinced she was that the Incorrigibles were about to make a gruesome snack of the poor wayward squirrel.

"I think I do understand," she answered slowly. "You mean that even when the outcome seems inevitable, something unexpected can still happen? And so it might be better not to know too much about what has been foretold so that one might keep an open mind, so to speak?"

Miss Mortimer nodded. "It is all too easy for most people to simply march in step toward whatever future they believe lies in store. But many forces shape a person's destiny, Penelope," she added. "And a prophecy made before you were born cannot take into account the greatest influence of all."

"Which is what?"

The headmistress smiled again. "You. Your own character. The kind of person you choose to be—and that you inspire others to be."

Penelope frowned. "Are you sure there is nothing more I can do, then?"

"Quite sure. Be brave and be true, be the best governess you can be, and give the future a chance to rewrite itself accordingly." Miss Mortimer gestured with her fork. "And be optimistic, Penny! For the unexpected does, quite frequently, happen. As the poet said, 'The best-laid plans of wolves and men gang aft agley.'"

"You mean mice," Penelope gently corrected. "Not wolves and men. Mice and men."

"Mice, mice, of course. How silly of me." Suddenly nervous, Miss Mortimer reached for her tea. Her hand trembled, but her voice remained firm. "Now, let us speak of this no more, and enjoy a marvelous meal. Tell me, have you begun reading the Giddy-Yap, Rainbow! books to the children yet? Heavens, I remember reading them to you, when you were scarcely bigger than Cassiopeia!"

THE FIDDLEHEADS PHILIPPE WAS FOLLOWED by fruit salad Philippe, fried fish Philippe, fettuccine and fennel Philippe, and numerous other courses, each one more tasty than the last.

Miss Mortimer scraped the last bite of fondue Philippe from her plate. "Genius," she said decisively. "Chef Philippe has truly outdone himself today, don't you agree?" She laid down her fork and dabbed her lips with the napkin. "Before I forget, Penelope, I have something for you."

Penelope was about to protest, for she had not thought to bring a gift for Miss Mortimer. But when she saw the small, familiar packet that Miss Mortimer removed from her reticule, she understood.

"I must ask that you continue to use the hair poultice I gave you." Miss Mortimer pressed it into Penelope's hands. "I brought you another packet so you will not run out."

The truth was, Penelope had not bothered to open the last packet of hair poultice that Miss Mortimer had sent. And, really—if the Incorrigibles were in some kind of danger, why waste time worrying about the condition of Penelope's scalp? But she knew her former headmistress well; for whatever reason, this business about Penelope's hair seemed to be a matter of real importance to Miss Mortimer, and there would be no argument.

"Do you promise to use it?" There was a teasing twinkle in Miss Mortimer's eye, but she was intent on securing Penelope's sworn promise. "On your honor, as a Swanburne girl?"

"Well, I suppose . . ."

"Promise me, Penelope."

"Yes, yes! I promise. I will use it." Penelope sighed. Though she was far from vain, the thought of returning to her former lackluster hair was not very appealing, especially after receiving that nice compliment from Simon Harley-Dickinson.

"Excellent. I know you will keep your word, Penelope, as you always have in the past." Miss Mortimer was already perusing the dessert menu. "Flan Philippe, figs in phyllo Philippe—everything sounds delectable. But when at the Fern Court, one must order the tarte Philippe. No other dessert compares. By the way, how do you like the *Hixby's Guide*?"

Penelope was in no mood for dessert. Both the meal and the conversation had been a great deal to absorb, and she was feeling quite overstuffed, in head, heart, and tummy.

"No, thank you; I am too full for tarte Philippe,

Miss Mortimer," she said politely. "As for the *Hixby's*, I am grateful for the gift, of course. Yet, I confess, I find it a curious volume. For example, it is supposed to be a guidebook to London, but the pictures all seem to be of Switzerland, or someplace similar. And a great many of the entries are in the form of little poems."

"That is curious." Miss Mortimer was still fixed on the dessert menu. "They say that the head bakers from the finest patisseries in Paris come to the Fern Court, take one bite of tarte Philippe, and collapse, weeping with envy."

Penelope sighed. "I think I will just have another cup of tea."

"No dessert? What is the matter, dear?" Miss Mortimer put the menu down. "You look pale and sad all of a sudden."

In fact, there was something troubling Penelope. It had occurred to her halfway through the frosted flakes Philippe, and now she was not sure how best to raise the subject, other than to simply plunge ahead. So she did.

"Miss Mortimer, as you know, it has been many years since"—the word "parents" felt so strange on her tongue she had to will herself to say it—"my parents left me in your care."

Penelope glanced down and saw that she was twisting her napkin into knots. "Perhaps they do not realize that I have already graduated. Perhaps they have lost track of time. But it is still possible that they intend to return for me, someday. And now that I have left Swanburne, I would not wish . . ." All at once Penelope found that her throat had tightened, and it was hard to speak. "I would not wish for them to come back looking for me and not find me there."

"Have no fear," Miss Mortimer said quickly. She, too, seemed to be misty-eyed all of sudden; perhaps it was a consequence of some errant fumes from the onion soup being served at another table. "I intend to remain headmistress at the Swanburne Academy for many a year to come. Should anyone of interest inquire as to your whereabouts, I will put you in touch with them directly."

Penelope nodded. "Thank you for your reassurance. That solves the matter completely."

It did not, of course. It had been more than ten years since Penelope had been deposited at Swanburne's doorstep. No letters, no birthday or Christmas presents—not even a picture postcard had arrived during that long span of time. Any ordinary person would have given up hope that the long-lost Lumleys ever intended to come back.

Of course, Penelope was far from ordinary. Much as a well-trained seal can keep one ball spinning on its shiny black nose while balancing another upon its tail, for all those years she, too, had managed to balance two somewhat contradictory beliefs: First, that, since her mother and father would undoubtedly come back for her one day, their long, unbroken silence was not something for her to feel lonesome or sad about; and second, that in the meantime, Penelope ought to go about her affairs exactly as if her parents were not in the picture at all, for, in fact, they were not.

It was not an easy trick, for the clever seal or the plucky young governess. But if there was one thing Penelope had learned from her headmistress, it was that worry, self-pity, and complaint were not how a Swanburne girl got through the day. Instead, just as one might use a ribbon to hold one's place in a fascinating book that one is temporarily forced to put down, Penelope simply made note of her confused and disappointed feelings and then put them gently to the side, for there was nothing to be done about them at present.

At the same time, she observed that the mere act of posing this question about her parents to Miss

Mortimer seemed to have lessened the heavy, burdened feeling inside her, the one she had assumed was the result of eating too much food Philippe.

"I believe I will have dessert after all," Penelope announced as she shook out her napkin, refolded it, and placed it neatly across her lap. "Followed by biscuits, and more tea. Shall I summon the waiter?"

THE NINTH CHAPTER

*The children visit the very last
place they should.*

WHEN THEY PARTED, Miss Mortimer gave Penelope precise directions for taking the omnibus so she would not have to walk all the way back to Number Twelve Muffinshire Lane.

Penelope had a great deal to think about along the way. There was the tarte Philippe, a dessert so indescribably delicious that Penelope found herself literally unable to describe it. And this business about the children being in danger was perplexing, to say the least—but, as Miss Mortimer had made clear, there was nothing for Penelope to do about it but continue being the good, careful governess she had already proven herself to be.

"Which is how I intended to proceed in any case," she thought, peering above a sea of hats to see where they had stopped, for the omnibus was crowded. "Though I am not sure I like Miss Mortimer's advice to not ask questions. After all, was it not Agatha Swanburne who said, 'The more one asks, the more one knows, and the more one knows, the more one asks'?"

Then there was her reluctant (oh, how reluctant!) promise about the hair poultice. Just when her hair was starting to attract compliments! Just when she had met a person of the male variety who might be inclined to notice such things! But a promise was a promise. Perhaps she ought to buy herself a new hat while in London. There were certainly many styles to choose from, judging from the array of plumed and beribboned specimens she could see bobbing and nodding around her.

"Or perhaps the poultice could wait a short while to be applied, just until we return to Ashton Place." The vehicle lurched its way 'round a corner so quickly the passengers swayed like trees in a storm. "For, being a gentleman, Mr. Harley-Dickinson is likely to offer to escort me to meet that Gypsy woman. It would only muddle things to alter my appearance now. After all, Miss Mortimer asked me to use the poultice; she did not specify when . . ."

Much as the omnibus proceeded in an orderly fashion from one stop to the next, Penelope, too, thought about all these different topics in turn—dessert, danger, hair, Simon—sorting them out as best she could, and then moving on. When she had finished her route, so to speak, and her mind was free to wander, Penelope found herself dwelling yet again upon the subject of her mother and father. Although obviously far from perfect, clearly, the Lumleys were not the absolute worst parents in the world. That title surely belonged to the parents of the Incorrigibles, whoever they were.

"At least *my* parents had the sense to leave me in the care of a well-regarded educational institution," Penelope told herself as she pictured her three pupils, barking and gnawing and baying at the moon. "*My* parents knew better than to abandon me in the woods to fend for myself, with only wild animals as my companions—pardon me!" she cried aloud suddenly. "Excuse me, driver! I believe we have reached my stop!"

As she alighted from the omnibus at the corner of Muffinshire Lane, Penelope was startled by a familiar yet enigmatic grunt.

"Good day, miss."

"Timothy!" she exclaimed (for Penelope was not so rude as to address the strange, watchful coachman as Old Timothy to his face). Then, without thinking, she blurted, "What are you doing here?"

He snorted. "I've just delivered Lord Fredrick Ashton to the humble cottage he's paid a king's ransom to rent. I trust that meets with your approval, governess."

"I apologize. I did not mean to speak so abruptly." Penelope quickly composed herself. "It surprises me to see you here in London. You seem so much a part of Ashton Place; it is jarring to think of you in town."

"People don't always stay where you put 'em, miss," he replied darkly. "As a governess, you ought to remember that."

His tone made Penelope shiver. "What do you mean?"

"Those children, for instance. You won't find them in the nursery where you left 'em, that's for sure." He turned and began walking back to the house with his quick, rolling gait. Penelope scurried after him.

"Excuse me! What do you mean, the children are

131

no longer in the nursery? I left them in Margaret's care, and I have only been gone an hour, or perhaps two. . . ." Though even as she said it, Penelope realized it had been closer to three hours since she had left the house. All that thought-provoking conversation and the culinary brilliance of Chef Philippe, not to mention the long walk to the Piazza Hotel and the bumpy ride back, had eaten up a substantial portion of the day.

"You've been gone three and one-quarter hours. Not that I've been keeping track." He looked straight ahead as they walked. "The children went on an excursion, with Margaret and some young fellow I never saw before."

Penelope's breath caught. "Do you mean Mr. Harley-Dickinson? Tall but not too tall, with gentle waves of brown hair, finely formed features, and the gleam of genius in his eye?" she said in a rush.

"Yup," the coachman grunted. "That's the one."

Misery! Simon had come, and she had missed him! And now he was out for the day with Margaret and the Incorrigibles! A pang of some unfamiliar feeling poked at her insides, someplace not too distant from her heart. It was like a dull, throbbing ache, or a sharp, twisty, stabbing feeling—oh, why were things becoming indescribable all of a sudden?

By now Old Timothy had gotten ten paces ahead of her. Once more she ran after him. "Please, one more question—do you happen to know where they went?" For she would not be content until she could see with her own eyes that all three children were safe and sound, and preferably doing something educational.

The coachman turned and looked at her with one eye half closed, and the other so wide open as to look as if it had just seen a ghost. "I believe they were going to the zoo."

"The *zoo*? But that is the very last place they ought to go!" Penelope cried.

"What's the trouble, miss? Most tykes love the zoo. Why should these three be any different?" Did Penelope imagine it, or was Old Timothy suppressing an evil chuckle? "Now I've a tasty errand to run. Here's my stop. Enjoy your day."

And with that he ducked into the nearest doorway, which Penelope saw was the entrance to a small shop called the Charming Little Bakery. Under different circumstances, and if she were not still feeling so spectacularly well fed, Penelope would have been interested in sampling the wares of this promising-sounding establishment. But her mind was fixed on the Incorrigibles.

"The zoo! Dear me, they could hardly have picked a worse place to go! I must find the children at once!" she resolved. But how exactly did one get to the zoo? The answer came in a flash.

"Miss Mortimer is proven right again: Having a guidebook is essential when visiting a strange city. I will dash up to the nursery and fetch my *Hixby's*. Surely it will contain directions to such a popular destination." With that, she lifted her skirt and broke into a run, and did not stop until she reached Number Twelve Muffinshire Lane.

THE SCIENCE-MINDED AMONG YOU WILL no doubt recall Newton's First Law of Motion, which (among other things) predicts that a distraught governess traveling at high speeds over a slippery surface will continue to do so until some greater force conspires to stop her. Mrs. Clarke had been right to scold Margaret; the wooden floors of the foyer had been polished to such a high degree of slickness that Penelope's feet flew out from beneath her the moment she burst through the door.

"Ah-*whoops*!" she cried, as most people would under the circumstances. Arms flailing, Penelope skidded down the hall on what the French would politely call her derriere, past the stairs and straight into the drawing room, where Newton's greater force lay ready and waiting: an overstuffed armchair containing the seated form of Sir Fredrick Ashton, the unimaginably wealthy and incurably nearsighted master of Ashton Place. Penelope slid almost completely beneath the chair before she finally came to a stop. Only her feet poked out from the back. Lord Ashton seemed oblivious to her arrival.

"Constance, can't you be more understanding? I've business to attend to. Men's business. And the club's accommodations are far more suitable for that sort of thing than this ridiculous frou-frou of a house, what?"

"But you have only just arrived! Really, Fredrick, it has been unbearably dull here. I have not set foot out of the house and have had no callers, not one! And there is no one to talk to except the servants."

"You mustn't talk to the servants, dear, unless you're ordering them about. It undermines your authority."

"What do expect me to do all day, then? Shop?"

"If you like. Just don't spend too much."

"But I thought the whole point of being rich was that nothing was too much!"

Thud.

"Ow!" Penelope yelped involuntarily, for she had bumped her head on the bottom of the chair in an attempt to crawl out from underneath.

"Did you hear something?" Lord Ashton looked behind him and on both sides of the chair. "Anybody back there? Stop or I'll shoot, ha ha ha!"

Unlike her husband, Lady Constance had eyesight enough to tell whether or not a set of human limbs was sticking out from beneath the furniture. She marched around the chair and planted both hands on her hips.

"And whose plain and sensible shoes are these?" she demanded. "The rest of you, come out at once!"

Meekly, Penelope pushed herself into view. "Pardon me," she said, clambering to her feet with as much dignity as she could muster, given the awkward circumstances.

Lord Ashton squinted in Penelope's direction. "See, there *was* someone there! Is it a burglar? No, wait, you're the governess, what?"

"Yes, Lord Ashton. I was on my upstairs to the nursery, and I, er, slipped. I apologize for the intrusion." She curtsied and started backing toward the door.

"Not so fast, Miss Lumley." Lady Constance had the look of a gathering storm. "Did you know the post has been delivered twice already today?"

"Why, yes. I imagine it has been." Penelope was unsure where this conversation might be headed, but

*"Did you hear something?" Lord Ashton looked
behind him and on both sides of the chair.*

she hoped it would be brief. The thought of the Incorrigible children at the zoo was still foremost in her mind, and she was determined to grab the *Hixby's Guide* and rescue them as soon as possible.

"Have you checked the mail tray, by any chance?"

"No, my lady." Penelope swallowed hard. "I have been out."

"I see." Lady Constance's voice was dangerously controlled. "If you could spare a moment from your busy social calendar to examine its contents, you will discover it contains yet another envelope addressed to you. Your letter has been lying there, taunting me, all day long!"

"I am sorry, Lady Constance—I did not intend—"

Lady Constance made a dramatic gesture to silence poor Penelope. "As if yesterday's impertinence was not enough! Once again, Miss Lumley, it seems you are *in receipt of mail.*"

"Mail? Zounds! I almost forgot." Lord Fredrick jumped to his feet and began patting his pockets. "Constance, dear, I've an invitation for you, somewhere. Baron Hoover handed it to me at the club; it's from his wife. Where did I put it? Maybe it will take your mind off spending my money for an afternoon, what? If I can find the blasted thing, that is . . ."

Lady Constance's mood changed on the instant. "An invitation? Really? Oh, Fredrick, that is the best news I have had since arriving in London! Hooray, hooray!"

"Wait . . . wait . . . here it is." From his vest pocket he removed a small envelope of heavy cream-colored stock. "Let that keep you busy for a while, eh? See you later, dear. Don't wait up."

He gave her an indifferent peck on the cheek and strode out of the room. Penelope, too, thought she might take the chance to leave. "Good day, ma'am," she murmured. She was nearly out the door when Lady Constance squealed and seized her by the arm.

"Oh, *look*! Do you see this envelope, Miss Lumley? This is from the Piazza Hotel! Simply the most exclusive hotel in London! Home of the Fern Court and the legendary Chef Philippe! I would not expect that someone of your social station would have heard of him, but trust me, he has no peer when it comes to the use of a whisk. They say he makes a positively indescribable dessert—"

"Tarte Philippe," offered Penelope, to move things along. Just imagining what might be going on at the zoo this very minute was more than she could stand— all those grim-faced bears, hungry lions, and wild-eyed baboons. . . .

"I beg your pardon?" Lady Constance looked stunned.

"Tarte Philippe, the indescribable dessert . . ." Penelope stopped, for it occurred to her that it might be wise to downplay her firsthand knowledge of this tasty treat. "That is only a wild guess, of course, given that the chef's name is Philippe." She smiled and shrugged, as if to say, "These crumbs on my skirt and the tiny fruit stain on my sleeve have nothing whatsoever to do with the actual tarte Philippe I greedily devoured not two hours ago."

Lady Constance gave Penelope a suspicious look but said only, "You are correct, Miss Lumley. Tarte Philippe is exactly what it is called. A lucky guess on your part, I suppose." She resumed her excited babble as she tore open the invitation. "Anyway, they say that tarte Philippe is so extraordinarily delicious that words . . . simply . . . fail . . ."

Her voice trailed off as she stared at the note. Her round eyes grew rounder, her pink pursed lips went slack. Then:

"What?" she yelped. "Is this some kind of a joke?" Lady Constance held the card between two fingertips as if it were a slimy object. "*This* is not an invitation to dine at the Piazza Hotel. *This* is an invitation to

140

accompany Baroness Hoover—not one of my favorites, by the way—on an excursion to the vilest, ugliest, dirtiest part of London! According to the baroness, tomorrow we are going to visit the poor!" Lady Constance spit out the word "poor" as if it were the seed of a rotten grape. "She claims such missions of mercy are all the rage among society ladies, and if I wish to fit in, I must go along."

Distraught, Lady Constance threw herself into Penelope's arms. "What a nightmare! With all the exquisite restaurants and dress shops in London, I am to spend my days performing acts of charity in a totally unfashionable and bad-smelling neighborhood! Oh, you have no idea how fortunate you are, Miss Lumley! For a person of your station would never think to aspire to luxuries such as dining at the Fern Court, and thus you do not have to endure the bitter disappointment when your hopes are all dashed to bits. It is an agony you are spared, lucky you!"

Penelope patted her mistress awkwardly on the back. "Perhaps the tarte Philippe is not all it is cracked up to be," she nearly said, for she did feel sorry for poor Lady Constance and wished to comfort her. But that would be dishonest, so instead she said, "Perhaps visiting the poor will not be as smelly as all that." This was a statement she could stand behind. After all, Penelope herself was once a Poor Bright Female, just like all the other girls at Swanburne, and she was quite sure she had never smelled of anything but plain soap and the occasional splash of lavender water.

"Don't be absurd. I can think of nothing more horrible. But I suppose it is better than sitting at home with nothing to do." Lady Constance righted herself, as if her teary-eyed dive at the bewildered governess had never happened. She sniffed and looked around the room. "Where are the bell pulls in this house? *Margaret!*" Then she turned to Penelope. "Find Margaret and send her to my dressing room at once. I must choose clothes for tomorrow. Something that makes me look generous."

"Margaret is not here, my lady," Penelope replied, unthinkingly. "She is at the zoo, with the children."

"The zoo?" Lady Constance's lip began to tremble once more. "Where is the justice in this world, I ask you? Governesses receiving mail! Ladies' maids taking trips to the zoo! While I, Lady Constance Ashton, will be forced to trudge through muck—and mire—and—*poor people*!"

Then the waterworks began in earnest. The wailing was so loud that Penelope had to fight the urge not to cover her ears. Luckily, the din attracted the notice of the staff, who came rushing to the rescue, and in the hubbub Penelope was finally able to run up to the nursery. By the time she returned with her *Hixby's Guide*, Lady Constance was surrounded by a dozen servants, who fanned her and waved smelling salts under her nose and offered tiny glasses of schnapps to revive her spirits.

"Even Dr. Westminster would have a hard time taming such a wild creature as Lady Constance," Penelope thought as she watched the scene unfold. "But speaking of wild creatures: to the zoo!"

THE TENTH CHAPTER

*Penelope rides a dandy-horse
and imagines it is a pony.*

IF YOU HAVE EVER BEEN forced to give directions, or fol-low them, you already know what a perfect muddle the whole business of navigation can be. One person's "go down the road a piece and bear left at the doughnut shop" is another's "proceed one-half mile and take the eastbound ramp." The innocent-sounding words "Yes, it's close enough to walk" can easily lure the unsuspecting tourist into an exhausting day-long climb, requiring supplemental oxygen, crampons, and a pickax. Put simply: $E = mc^2$. Put even more simply: Everything is relative, including time and space, both of which are essential to finding one's way around town.

This is why sailors, who quite understandably worry more than most other people do about getting lost at sea, prefer to navigate by the stars. But the stars themselves are far from fixed; they wheel through space at such unimaginable velocities that to seriously ponder the subject puts one at risk of dizzy spells and a nasty headache. The brave sailors manage nevertheless.

As for Miss Penelope Lumley, she had neither sextant nor astrolabe. Her only means of transport was pluck, courage was the fuel that propelled her, and her North Star was determination. The Incorrigible children were in danger, and she simply had to save them, right now, no arguments.

In that unstoppable, Swanburnian spirit, she opened the *Hixby's Guide*, flipped at once to the index (truly, one of the most useful features of any book), and quickly found the entry marked, "Zoo, London, pp. 66–68 (inclusive)."

"This will tell me exactly what I wish to know," she assured herself in a burst of optimism. However, there are times when all the optimism in the world comes to naught, and this was one of those times, for pages 66–68 (inclusive) contained only pictures of animals with identifying captions. There was a pretty songbird labeled a snow lark and a gray-furred rodent called an alpine marmot. To Penelope it looked like a sort of overgrown mountain squirrel.

As for directions, there were none—until, beneath a picture of an elephant, Penelope found this aromatically themed verse:

The way to the zoo your nose will tell,
For elephants are not hard to smell.

"Smelling elephants? That is not much to go on," Penelope thought. She scoured the surrounding pages for any tidbit that might offer more practical guidance (a street address would have been ideal), but found only a drawing of an ibex, a large goat with a flinty gaze and enormous curved horns that looked very pointy indeed.

What to do? Despite her breathing exercises, Penelope felt a rising panic. If only she had a pony, like Edith-Anne Pevington! Of course she did not know how to ride, for without a pony of her own to practice on she had had scant opportunity to learn. Even so, she could easily imagine how thrilling it would be to leap onto Rainbow's back and gallop off to rescue the Incorrigibles from those lethal ibex horns and the razor-sharp buckteeth of crazed mountain squirrels.

"That settles it. When we return to Ashton Place, I must learn to ride at the earliest opportunity," she resolved. Penelope had gone off on a bit of a tangent, but it was a lucky tangent, for the idea of learning to ride led her to another, more immediately useful idea—one that might actually help solve her current dilemma.

"Young man!" She yelled through cupped hands. "You there, in the tweed cap! May I borrow your velocipede?"

"You mean, my dandy-horse?" The boy, who looked not much older than Alexander, was riding up and down Muffinshire Lane on a two-wheeled invention that nowadays would be best described as a bicycle without pedals, propelled in scooterlike fashion by the feet of the rider. "Nah! Get your own."

This lack of civic-mindedness was discouraging, yet Penelope made another attempt. "Young man! I am in urgent need of transportation. The safety of three small children is in question. Surely you could lend me your vehicle a short while, for their sake?"

He came to a stop in front of her. "All right. How much?"

Penelope may have been in urgent need of transportation, but she was no fool. "I did not ask to buy your velocipede; I asked to borrow it," she replied sternly. "However, if payment is required, please note that I am a professional governess. I could give you lessons. Latin, geometry, art appreciation, fundamentals of architecture, basic veterinary skills—choose whatever subject you like. Just lend me the dandy-horse."

"Lessons?" He made a face. "Nah! You'd have to pay me!"

Penelope was quite taken aback. "Forgive me for saying so, but that is no way to speak about your own education. You would do well to heed the words of Agatha Swanburne—you have heard of Agatha Swanburne, haven't you?"

"Nah! Why? Is she famous?"

"I should say she is!" Penelope was losing patience, but she was also beginning to feel sorry for this urchin. "Agatha Swanburne was a very wise woman who once said, 'Few would waste a perfectly good sandwich, so why waste a perfectly good mind?' Now, will you reconsider my offer?"

The boy thought for a minute. "Nah!" He pushed off again and rode in tight circles around her. "But I wouldn't mind a sandwich."

"A sandwich it shall be, then." She dug into her purse. "There is a charming little bakery down the street, called the Charming Little Bakery. You may go there and eat to your heart's content, as much as this many coins will buy." She placed the money in his hand. "In exchange, I ask that you lend me your veloci-pede for—well, for as long as it is required."

He stared in wonder at his coin-filled palm. "A bak-ery? Crikey! Sure, lady, take the dandy-horse. Ain't mine anyhow."

He hopped off the seat and skittered away to the bakery, leaving Penelope in possession of what she now suspected was a stolen velocipede. But no matter; how to operate the vehicle was the far more urgent question. Riding sidesaddle did not seem to be an option, so she tucked up her long skirt around both legs in order to perch on the seat. Since she had recently skated across a hard wooden floor on her bottom, the extra padding was more than welcome.

"What a curious invention," Penelope thought as she turned the handlebars this way and that, just to get the feel of it. "The addition of a simple gear mecha-nism and foot pedals to propel the wheels would make it far more efficient. Still, it will be faster than walking. *Allons, mes amis!*"

Penelope's optimism had returned in full force. After all, she had seen the boy riding, and it looked straightforward enough. One simply pushed one's feet along the ground while balancing upon the seat. She merely had to summon the courage to begin . . . right . . . left . . . right . . . left . . . now a little faster, right-left-right-left, *rightleftrightleftrightleft* . . .

"Giddy-yap, Rainbow!" she cried aloud, to bolster her nerve, and also to warn any passersby of her wobbly, swerving approach. "Gallop on, my brave pony! There will be sweet carrots in it for you when we get back to the barn!"

Penelope rapidly picked up speed. "Why, this is not difficult at all," she thought, perhaps feeling a bit more confident than she had a right to. "And I will wager that Mr. Hixby's advice is sounder than it first appeared. I shall ride until I smell elephants! For that will mean the zoo must surely be nearby." This is the trouble with optimism, you see: In excess, it makes even ridiculous ideas seem worth a try. And the chance to put this one to the test had arrived, for Penelope was already careening toward the intersection.

"Easy as pie!" she thought, preparing to sniff. "One direction will smell more like elephants than the other, and that is the direction in which I shall go." And with

"Giddy-yap, Rainbow!" she cried aloud . . .

that, she closed her eyes.

You may well wonder why she did this, but the truth is most people tend to close their eyes when trying to get a good whiff of something. If you perform this experiment at home (using all necessary safety precautions, of course), you will amazed at the way that shutting off one sense instantly sharpens the rest.

Even so, closing one's eyes is never a good idea while attempting to steer a velocipede through a busy intersection. Moreover, no matter how deeply Penelope inhaled, it was not immediately apparent which direction smelled more like elephants. She sniffed and sniffed, but as they say nowadays, it was a toss-up.

"My sense of smell may not be up to the job, but my hearing is as keen as an owl's," Penelope thought, still riding blindly. "I hear voices shouting, a sharp crack of the whip, horses neighing in protest, the clatter of hooves, the skid of carriage wheels, the Incorrigibles calling, 'Lumawoo'—whoops!"

"Lumawoo! Lumawoo!"

"Whoa! Whoa, I say!"

"Easy, Rainbow," Penelope cried, for the velocipede seemed to be rearing up in alarm. It skidded out from under her; the next thing she knew, she was sprawled on the cobblestones of Muffinshire Lane.

The elephants would have to wait. She opened her eyes and found herself face-to-face with the tall spoked wheel of a luxurious town coach, which had come to a sudden stop not three feet from where she lay. Looking in the other direction, she saw that the coach was pulled by four spirited, pure black Andalusians. The elegant carriage was the same midnight shade as the horses, so richly polished it gleamed in the sun.

The coachman stared down at her. Beads of sweat studded his forehead. His hands were still white-knuckled from hauling back on the reins.

"What were you thinking, miss?" he scolded. "Taking some sort of a joy ride? You nearly killed us all, there!"

Four long, dark horse faces, with their rubbery lips and swiveling ears, and annoyed expressions in their long-lashed eyes, also turned 'round to look at her, snorting and huffing as if to say, *"Neigh, neigh!* Why don't you look where you're going, Miss Two Legs? And get a real pony while you're at it. That dandy-horse contraption is perfectly ridiculous!"

"Miss Two Legs? Why, that is not a very polite form of address," Penelope mumbled in reply. Understand that she was more than a little disoriented, for she had taken quite a tumble.

"Lumawoo! Lum*ahwooooooooo!*" The three Incorrigible children howled her name from someplace close by. A high, squeaking sound accompanied them; it might have been Margaret's voice, but in Penelope's mind it sounded more like the chirruping of a worried Nutsawoo.

"Say! Are you all right, Miss Lumley?" A familiar and perfectly nice young face, waves of brown hair, finely formed features, gleam of genius and all, gazed down at her and extended a hand.

Now she was quite sure she must have a concussion. For here was Simon Harley-Dickinson gently helping her to her feet, and the Incorrigibles, their faces grubby and hands sticky from candy, clambering out of the town coach and crowding anxiously around her. Beowulf clutched a balloon on a string, and all three children smelled, frankly, like elephants.

"Simon? I mean, Mr. Harley-Dickinson, of course. Forgive me, I am still a bit flustered from the fall. . . ." Penelope blinked, and blinked again. Muffinshire Lane was whirling like a top, but the children hugged her so hard she could not have toppled over again if she wanted to, which, naturally, she did not.

"Say, that's some set of wheels you have there, Miss Lumley!" Simon grinned from ear to ear.

Penelope hid her embarrassment by vigorously brushing the dirt off her tangled skirt. "What, the velocipede?" she said offhandedly. "It is perfectly easy, once you get the knack." She looked around once more. Her head was beginning to clear, and the street had stopped spinning. Only then did the import of the situation dawn on her fully. "But—wait!" She turned to the Incorrigibles. "I thought you were at the zoo! In fact, I was just on my way to find you there. I was afraid something dreadful might have happened."

The children only giggled and took turns batting at Beowulf's balloon. Penelope hid her enormous relief by sounding cross. "Alexander! Beowulf! Cassiopeia! I would like an explanation, please. What were you doing, riding in this magnificent carriage? And to whom does it belong? I am quite sure I have told you never to accept rides from strangers—or if I have not, I should have, and will do so frequently from this point forward."

"But I am not a stranger, of course." A tall, middle-aged man swung gracefully out of the carriage. He, too, was dressed in black, and his hair was as dark as the quartet of horsetails that were now impatiently whipping about. "We were at the zoo, Miss Lumley, and we are just on our way back. The carriage is mine.

I am glad you find it pleasing."

That voice! It was rich, powerful—and familiar. She would have recognized it even with her eyes closed, but there could be no mistaking the imposing, black-clad figure who stood before her.

It was Judge Quinzy. She remembered him vividly from the holiday ball at Ashton Place. She had met many of Lord Fredrick's powerful friends that night, and frankly she did not care for any of them; she found them stuck-up and rude. The men in particular had showed a fixation on hunting animals that, in Penelope's worst imaginings, nearly threatened to encompass the "wild wolf children" Lord Fredrick had bragged about finding on his property. Judge Quinzy had been the only one who had shown a more human interest in Penelope, and in the Incorrigibles. Oddly, that made her like him the least of all.

"Judge Quinzy! I beg your pardon." She gave a quick curtsy, and almost lost her balance.

"A pleasure to see you again, Miss Lumley." He smiled. "What a splendid day we had! Didn't we, children?"

They children nodded in agreement. Instinctively, Penelope put a protective arm around her three pupils. "Forgive my rudeness, Your Honor, but I am confused.

How did you come to take the children to the zoo?"

"A happy accident," he answered with a shrug. "When I heard that my dear friends the Ashtons were in residence in London, I came by to pay a call. But when I arrived, Lady Ashton was at the hairdresser, and Lord Ashton had not yet arrived. However, this charming young lady"—at which Margaret giggled shrilly—"was entertaining the children near the front door. They were quite impossible to miss."

"We were playing at ice-skating, Miss," Margaret squeaked in explanation. "The floor's rather slippery there, I'm afraid."

"Naturally, my first thought was of you, Miss Lumley," the judge went on. "At once I inquired if you were still employed by the Ashtons—I would have been sorely disappointed if you were not, for you know how impressed I was by your three pupils when I met them at Christmas. But Margaret told me the children were only in her care for the afternoon, for you had gone to have lunch with a friend. I do hope it was a pleasant rendezvous," he added, smooth as silk.

"It was, Your Honor," she said, but inside she was seething. How dare he insinuate anything of that sort! And with Simon standing right there!

Judge Quinzy gestured behind him. "My carriage

is large, as you see. And it seemed too fine a day to stay indoors skating around the floor in one's stocking feet, don't you agree?" The children demonstrated their skating techniques, and Judge Quinzy chuckled warmly.

"His Honor even said I should take the afternoon off and enjoy myself while he took the children to the zoo, and he'd square it with Lady Ashton personally, but I'd given my word to watch the three young'uns, so I wouldn't dream of it," Margaret said proudly. "But I do wish you'd been with us, Miss Lumley. I've never been to a zoo park before! It was more fun than—well, a barrel of monkeys. We left a note in the mail tray for you, hoping you'd come."

"I arrived just as the children were climbing aboard this noble coach of polished ebony, if you don't mind the poetical language. My muse seems to be back in full force." To Penelope, Simon quietly added, "I got your letter about that Gypsy fortune-teller. A strange business! I came straight over."

Penelope thought she saw Judge Quinzy's right eyebrow arch momentarily, but he quickly composed himself. "The children were so delighted to see Mr. Harley-Dickinson, naturally I invited him to join our expedition," the judge explained.

Perhaps she was still discombobulated from the fall, but Penelope had a nagging sense that Judge Quinzy's tale did not quite add up. "What an exciting day you had, children," she said briskly as she looked each child over in turn. "You will have to tell me all about it—after you take your baths, that is," she said, crinkling her nose, for the elephant smell was really quite pronounced.

"Educashawoo," Alexander agreed. Beowulf was too busy examining the velocipede to comment. Cassiopeia looked up at her governess and laughed. "Messy apples!" she said, indicating Penelope's head.

Embarrassed, Penelope reached up to smooth her hair, which had started the day in its usual neat bun, but was now in a state of wind-whipped disarray. "Thank goodness for my hatpin," she thought as she tucked the loose strands back under her hat, which had miraculously stayed on during her wild velocipede ride. (As Agatha Swanburne once said, "A nice sharp hatpin has many uses; no woman should leave home without one," but it was a private comment made to a close relative, which explains why Penelope was unfamiliar with the remark.)

Judge Quinzy looked as if he was about to say something. He did not. However, Penelope felt him watching her with a strange intensity, rendered all the stranger by the way his thick glasses magnified his eyes. It made her self-conscious, and she finished tucking in her hair as quickly as she could.

"Lumawoo, see. Postcards from zoo!" Cassiopeia announced, waving a fistful of them.

"My heavens! You have chimpanzees, and panthers, and baboons, and even a hippopotamus. Nutsawoo will be thrilled." Then Penelope frowned. "Cassiopeia, how did you pay for those?"

The little girl pointed at Judge Quinzy.

"Your Honor, I must protest," Penelope said firmly. "Taking the children to the zoo was already much too generous. You certainly did not have to buy postcards." Penelope almost added, "for a squirrel," but stopped herself just in time.

"Thankawoo," Cassiopeia said sweetly to the judge. "Thankawoo very much."

Judge Quinzy patted her on the head. "You are very welcome, Miss Incorrigible." He turned to Penelope. "And you are too kind, Miss Lumley. I am not nearly as generous as you believe. You see, a man in my position is expected to busy himself with serious pursuits. It can be rather dull, I'm afraid. I was grateful for the excuse to visit the zoo, since I have no children of my own."

Penelope nodded, understanding. And yet, she thought a few moments later, there was something about the way Judge Quinzy helped Beowulf onto the velocipede, and then held on as the boy got his bearings and began to scoot 'round and 'round the carriage, laughing, while the judge clapped his hands and called out phrases of encouragement, that—in her admittedly limited experience of such things—could only be described as fatherly.

THE ELEVENTH CHAPTER

In the aftermath of adventure,
a friendship is forged.

NOWADAYS, PEOPLE RESORT to all kinds of activities in order to calm themselves after a stressful event: performing yoga poses in a sauna, leaping off bridges while tied to a bungee, killing imaginary zombies with imaginary weapons, and so forth. But in Miss Penelope Lumley's day, it was universally understood that there is nothing like a nice cup of tea to settle one's nerves in the aftermath of an adventure—a practice many would find well worth reviving.

As you might imagine, Penelope was now in sore

need of just such a soothing cuppa, and the Incorrigible children were in sore need of baths; truly, the scent of elephants was so distinctive that Mr. Hixby may have had a point, after all. So back to Number Twelve Muffinshire Lane they marched, after bidding Judge Quinzy good day and offering more thanks for his kindness, all of which he grandly waved off.

Penelope felt she owed a debt to Margaret, too. If not for the young housemaid's sense of duty—and Simon's timely arrival, of course—the children might have been whisked off to spend the day alone with Judge Quinzy, an uncomfortable notion at best. It spoke so well of Margaret's character that Penelope wondered if she, too, had been influenced by the wisdom of Agatha Swanburne somewhere along the way.

She tried to say as much, but the humble girl just giggled and squeaked, "No need for all that, miss! I was just minding the children, like I said I would. If you'll pardon me, I'd best get back to work. Mrs. Clarke will be lookin' for me." She bobbed a quick curtsy and raced back to the house. Now that Penelope had returned, Margaret would spend the rest of this lovely day cleaning fireplace grates, sweeping carpets, and tending to the whims of her high-strung mistress whenever Lady Constance rang the bell.

"Poor Margaret," Penelope thought as she watched the good-hearted girl skitter gracefully away across the cobblestones. "I hope Lady Constance does not scold her for going to the zoo. If she does, it will be my fault for mentioning it. And poor Lady Constance! I wonder if she knows how vexing people find her?"

Vexing, indeed! Even as she had the thought, Penelope wished she might invite Simon in for tea and a few of the biscuits that the children had begged her to buy at the Charming Little Bakery. (While paying for her purchase, she was saddened, but not wholly surprised, to overhear the baker complaining: Apparently a young boy had stolen two loaves of rye bread and a half dozen sticky buns before making a fast getaway, not twenty minutes earlier.)

But Penelope knew that if Lady Constance saw her entertaining an actual caller—and a young gentleman, mind you!—there would be no end to the hysteria.

Instead Penelope and Simon strolled at a leisurely pace, while the children took turns scooting beside them on the velocipede. Cassiopeia was much too small for her feet to reach the ground, so her brothers had to steady her and push her along, but they did not seem to mind.

Penelope was eager to ask Simon about the

fortune-teller, but first she simply had to know what had happened at the zoo, and so she asked him to tell her the story.

"Really, the children were remarkable," Simon began as they walked. "I've got a soft spot for animals myself—"

"Do you? So do I!" Penelope knew it was rude to interrupt, but his statement pleased her so greatly that the words burst out of her. She almost added, "Especially for ponies," but she was not sure whether her exhortations to Rainbow while riding the velocipede had been overheard by Simon, so she omitted that detail for now.

"You do? Fancy that." He, too, sounded pleased. "Anyway, I'm usually able to make friends with even the most skittish beasts. Runs in the family. My great-uncle Pudge, the sailor, tells the story of how he cozied up to an albatross once, out at sea—but honestly, the children showed a knack for it the likes of which I've never seen. They even helped give some medicine to a sick elephant."

At the word "elephant," the children started galumphing around, laughing and making loud trumpeting noises. Simon looked abashed. "I hope it doesn't frighten you to hear what happened, Miss Lumley. As you can see, nobody got hurt." Penelope reassured him, and his voice grew thrillingly dramatic as he told what happened next:

"When we arrived at the elephant cage, the zoo-keeper was at his wit's end trying to persuade the ailing pachyderm to take his pill. Before anyone could stop them, the children scrambled over the bars! Beowulf shimmied up the elephant's trunk to hold it out of the way. Cassiopeia petted his great gray knee to calm the beast, and Alexander calmly took the pill from the zoo-keeper and popped it down the elephant's gullet, one two three." The children happily acted out the scene as he described it, using the velocipede as a stand-in for the elephant.

"Bravo! What an adventure you had! And it also explains the smell. But children, remember, climbing into zoo cages is not something to make a habit of. I hope you will keep that in mind." Privately, of course, Penelope was very proud of the Incorrigibles for rushing to the aid of a sick animal, for it is just what she would have done, no matter how many iron bars were in the way.

She waited until the children had scooted out of earshot again before asking, "Mr. Harley-Dickinson, tell me: Did the children show any fright when faced with more familiar, forest-dwelling-type creatures?

Bears, for example? Or"—her voice wavered as she said it—"wolves?"

"Oh, we never saw the Wildlife of Great Britain exhibit. It was closed for repairs," Simon explained. "Judge Quinzy was keenly disappointed about that. But we amused ourselves nicely with the giraffes and orangutans and whatnot. The children couldn't get enough of them. They pointed and laughed as if they'd never seen anything so funny."

"How interesting," Penelope observed to herself. "To the Incorrigible children, these exotic beasts must have been as strange and comical looking as a person in a clown costume would be to the average child." But to Simon she only said, "It sounds like everyone had a marvelous time."

Simon gave her a curious look. "Forgive me for noticing, Miss Lumley, but you don't seem very surprised by my zoo story. Maybe I've got it wrong, but I suspect the average governess would have a conniption fit at the hair-raising tale I've just portrayed." He frowned. "Or perhaps I failed to capture the death-defying drama of it all? I hope my muse hasn't left me again."

Penelope felt her cheeks flush. Even though it seemed as if they had known each other for ages, in reality, her acquaintance with Simon was still so new that she had not yet mentioned the fact that the children had been raised by wolves. Was now an appropriate time? Penelope had read all the etiquette books in the Swanburne library, but she could not recall a rule that applied specifically to this situation.

"I assure you, Mr. Harley-Dickinson, your zoo story was nothing short of riveting, and I would hear it again in a heartbeat. But the children have a somewhat unusual background," she said cautiously. "It tends to make them highly skilled with animals. I have observed it myself, and that is why I am not surprised by your tale."

"Unusual background?" Simon stopped walking and turned to Penelope. "That's just what Judge Quinzy said. He's a curious fellow. Wanted to know all about me, how I'd made your acquaintance, and what I thought of the children. I told him three more clever and charming tykes I'd not had the pleasure of meeting. 'But what do you make of their unusual background?' he said. 'Well,' I replied, 'it *is* unusual; not every child gets to roll around in piles of money like they do at Ashton Place. But as long as that sensible Miss Lumley's in charge, it shouldn't completely ruin them.'" Simon grinned. "Hizzoner guffawed nonstop for a minute and a half after that one. Say, what *did* he mean by it? Were they in the circus?"

The Incorrigibles were still busy playing with the velocipede. Penelope wondered how much she ought to reveal, but one look at Simon's perfectly nice face made up her mind. Quickly she told him all she knew about the children's "unusual background."

Now it was his turn to be riveted. "Raised by wolves! You don't say," he exclaimed when she was done. "I'd write a play about it, but no one'd believe me."

And then, because she simply had to trust someone, she told Simon everything: all about the strange goings-on at Ashton Place, the mysterious danger that Miss Mortimer had warned her about, and the fortune-teller's bizarre words, "The hunt is on." The only part she left out, in fact, was Miss Mortimer's request that she not investigate the matter further. For truly, what harm could come of satisfying her curiosity?

"So you see, Mr. Harley-Dickinson," she concluded, "that is why I must speak with that Gypsy. Unlikely as it seems, the semitoothless soothsayer may know something about what lies beneath all these confounding events."

Simon shook his head. "I'm afraid I've got bad news for you, Miss Lumley. I haven't seen Madame Ionesco for days—not since the day I met you and the children, in fact."

Penelope could scarcely conceal her disappointment. "Is it unusual for her to be absent for so long?"

"A bit, yes. She's usually busy prognosticating all over the neighborhood. You'd be amazed what people will pay for a glimpse of the Great Unknown."

"I hope no terrible fate has befallen her," Penelope said, alarmed. "Or are people in her profession able to foresee such calamities and avoid them?"

Simon shrugged. "Wish I knew. But even a fortune-teller's entitled to a holiday now and then. Perhaps she's taken a trip out of town. If you like, tomorrow you and the children can come by my garret for a visit, and we can take a look 'round the neighborhood for her. Afterward I'll show you some of my theatrical haunts. 'The life of a bard revealed,' and all that. Say, there's a new show opening at the Drury Lane. If we play our cards right, the stage manager will let us in to watch a rehearsal."

A show! Penelope found the idea far more exciting than she dared let on. "That would be amusing," she remarked, trying to sound casual. "And tomorrow Lady Constance will be out all day visiting the poor, which means we may come and go—" She could have said, "without provoking a ridiculous tantrum," but that would have been unkind. "Without disturbing her," she finished.

"Visiting the poor? Say, that's admirable. This Lady Constance must be a good egg, as rich ladies go."

Penelope suppressed a smile, for she had not yet given up hopes of befriending Lady Constance. "You are very kind to say so," she answered, quite sincerely. "In any case, we would be delighted to join you. The tour you propose sounds highly educational."

"Or educashawoo, as the Incorrigibles would call it. Cute, the way they do that. Makes a bit more sense, now that I know about the wolf business. Here we are at Number Twelve again. You probably didn't notice, but we've completed five full circumnavigations of Muffinshire Lane. Captain Cook himself couldn't have done better." Simon pulled at his collar and scuffed his feet on the ground once more. "I suppose I should have mentioned it earlier, but it was too pleasant a conversation to stop walking so soon."

"Five! Really?" Penelope exclaimed playfully, for of course she had noticed. "It is a credit to your navigational skills that we did not blow off course."

Simon rubbed the back of his neck. "All right, then. I'll pick you up, say, eleven o'clockish—or would you rather use that fine guidebook of yours to lead you to the West End?"

"You mean, the *Hixby's*?" Penelope sighed in frustration. "A tall man with a green feather on his sleeve tried to steal it on the train on our way to London. The children stopped him just in time. Now I am almost beginning to wish he *had* stolen it, for it has proven to be of very little use."

Again, Penelope stopped herself in the nick of time, for she could easily have added, "Imagine, trying to find my way to the zoo by following the smell of elephants!" But of course that would require quite a bit of explaining.

She took the guidebook from her purse and showed it to Simon. "See? The only entry that contains any useful information at all is the one about Gallery Seventeen, at the British Museum."

"Overuse of Symbolism in Minor Historical Portraits," he read, thumbing through the pages. "Say, look at that! Eight pages of detailed commentary, hours of operation, admission fees, schedule of holidays, a scale drawing of the museum . . ." Turning the volume sideways, he added, "And a fold-out map of how to get there, complete with latitude and longitude."

He shut the book and handed it back to Penelope.

"Impressive. I'd say this Hixby fellow is dead set on getting people to visit Gallery Seventeen."

"I share your conclusion, Mr. Harley-Dickinson. But I do find it ironic." Penelope traced the illustration on the book's cover with her fingertip; it was a small, pretty white flower. "For he describes Gallery Seventeen as 'obscure and little trafficked,' yet the guidebook makes such a to-do about going there, surely it must be overrun with visitors by now. Unless . . ."

Much as a well-trained pony might jump over a murky brook and land, dry hooved, in the sun-dappled meadow beyond, Penelope's mind now made a sudden leap over the muddle. "Mr. Harley-Dickinson, do you happen to know where all the bookstores in London are located?" She was so excited by her flash of insight that she could hardly keep from clapping her hands.

"You bet I do," he proudly replied. "Every last one of 'em."

Penelope felt the deep satisfaction one can only enjoy when in the company of a kindred spirit. "How marvelous!" she exclaimed. Her mind raced, and her words tumbled out willy-nilly. "The children are much too tired for another outing. I dare not leave them again, and in any case, they have not yet finished their

173

essays on the causes and consequences of the Peloponnesian War."

"Athens versus Sparta? I'm not sure I follow—"

She lowered her voice to a more confidential tone. "If you are willing, after we part I would ask that you go at once and visit as many bookstores as you possibly can. See if you find even one other copy of the *Hixby's Guide to London*. Or any other Hixby's guide, for that matter."

"Easy enough." Simon saluted as if he were already on his way. "But why?"

"Because I now suspect *this*," Penelope said as she laid a hand on the book's cover, "is the only copy of *Hixby's Lavishly Illustrated Guide to London: Compleat with Historical Reference, Architectural Significance, and Literary Allusions* in existence."

"Now, that is a fascinating and peculiar notion." Simon stroked his chin, which he had shaved for the first time that very morning. "But if you're right, what do you suppose it means?"

"It means that I, Miss Penelope Lumley, am the singular person whom the author of this volume hopes to lure to that obscure and little-trafficked Gallery Seventeen." She glanced around to make sure the children could not overhear. "It would also mean that Miss

Mortimer knows far more than she has told me—for it was she who sent me the guidebook to begin with."

"Then she must know who made it," Simon exclaimed.

"Exactly," Penelope agreed. "And, perhaps, why someone would try to steal it."

At that point Beowulf scooted up to show Penelope and Simon a new trick he had invented on the velocipede (he called it "popping a wheelawooo"), and that kept them occupied for another circumnavigation of Muffinshire Lane.

It also gave Simon an idea. Lacking a horse or cart, Simon suggested that it would greatly speed his efforts to visit every bookstore in London if he rode the velocipede himself. "If the children don't mind parting with it, of course," he said, tipping his hat to them.

The Incorrigibles had no objection to letting Simon take the velocipede. It had been a long day, and now it was time to bathe and eat supper and hear the rest of that funny Scottish poem about the mouse, which they liked so much that just thinking about it started all three of them drooling—or possibly it was the idea of a tasty wee mousie that caused the saliva to flow. In any case, they were eager to hear more.

But Penelope had another concern. "Mr. Harley-Dickinson, I must be frank with you," she said solemnly.

"I do not know to whom the velocipede properly belongs."

"Was it lost?"

Penelope thought of the two loaves of rye bread and half dozen sticky buns. "More likely stolen, I fear."

"Better not tell me about it, then. The less I know, the less they can make me confess on the rack." It took her a moment to realize he was joking.

"But is it wise to tour London on a stolen velocipede?" she asked worriedly. Make no mistake: The Swanburne Academy for Poor Bright Females was an excellent and highly regarded school, but this was the sort of question that Penelope's education had utterly failed to address. "For what if you are caught? The officers of the law will surely think that you are the thief."

"Contraband, eh?" Simon chuckled and hopped easily onto the seat. "This is getting positively dramatic! Don't worry, Miss Lumley, I'll be careful and steer clear of constables. Besides, I've a new friend who's a judge, remember? If that can't keep a fellow out of the lockup, nothing can."

"Good luck, then. Oh, Mr. Harley-Dickinson! Do take a biscuit for the road." She offered one from the charming little tin the bakery had provided.

"Custard cream! My favorite. Thanks, Miss Lumley." He took one and popped it in his mouth. With that, he was off.

AND SO, JUST AS IT was on the first day they met, (which, of course, had been only a few days before, though it truly seemed much longer), Miss Penelope Lumley and Mr. Simon Harley-Dickinson had bid each other farewell at the steps of Number Twelve Muffinshire Lane. Except this time Penelope knew exactly when she would see Mr. Harley-Dickinson again, and it would be quite soon. The very next day, in fact!

Not only that, but she felt Simon had proven himself someone whom she could trust and rely upon to help think things through. Despite all the days' mysteries, riddles, and conundrums, the realization that, in Simon, she had found a true friend, was enough to cheer Penelope to the core. As Agatha Swanburne once said, "When things are looking up, there's no point in looking elsewhere."

And a true friend was a treasure beyond price. This Penelope knew from *The New Pony*, a lovely, early story that showed how young Edith-Anne Pevington and her new pony colt, Rainbow, first came to understand and love each other, despite a few blunders at the start—for how was Edith-Anne to know that Rainbow much preferred carrots to sugar cubes, and could only stand to have his hooves cleaned if she sang to him while she worked?

Just thinking about it prompted Penelope to start humming the wordless little sea chantey that Simon had been whistling earlier.

"Apples, apples, apples." Cassiopeia sang along as Penelope vigorously shampooed the child's head. The elephant smell had proved stubborn and required serious scrubbing. The boys had already taken their baths; at the moment they were busy adding pictures of antique Grecian helmets, weaponry, and naval vessels to their journals. Penelope had given up trying to convince them to use the journals as an accurate record of their stay in London; if Nutsawoo believed they had spent the time engaged in sea battles with the Spartan fleet, what harm could it do?

"Bubble apples, bubble apples!" Cassiopeia gave a little tug to the end of her governess's hair, which now hung loose around her shoulders, as it was late in the day and Penelope had already taken out the pins.

"Lumawoo apples, là la la!" Cassiopeia made a soapy mustache of her own hair and Penelope's, and then blew through the strands until soap bubbles floated lazily through the air. The colors of the two strands of hair really were nearly identical.

"Close your eyes, dear, that's a good girl." Penelope rinsed the soap away with a pitcher of fresh water and wondered: Did the similarity in her hair color and the children's have anything to do with Miss Mortimer's urgent request that Penelope use the hair poultice?

First the *Hixby's Guide*, now this! Penelope certainly did not want to feel cross with Miss Mortimer, but she wished her headmistress had been a bit more forthcoming. Perhaps it would be wisest to simply follow her instructions and use the poultice at once.

Of course, Penelope was going to see Simon the next day. Was it silly that she wanted to look her best? Surely the poultice could wait awhile longer? But then she remembered the way Judge Quinzy had stared at her that afternoon, as she had tucked the loose strands of hair away under her hat. Had he noticed the similarity as well? If so, why would it matter? Such coincidences happened all the time.

"In any event, I ought not to worry about Simon," Penelope concluded, for a true friend would not care one way or the other what shade her hair was. Of that she was certain.

As for Judge Quinzy . . . perhaps she had imagined

him looking at her hair. But it jogged her memory. There had been something about his story that had troubled her; what was it?

As she squeezed the water out of Cassiopeia's hair, it came to her. The hairdresser! He said he had come to the house to see Lord and Lady Ashton, but Lady Ashton had been at the hairdresser.

But Lady Constance had not left the house. And had had no callers, either; Penelope had heard her say as much to Lord Fredrick.

Why would Judge Quinzy lie about something like that?

"Cassawoof poem, please," the dripping girl requested as Penelope lifted her out of the hip bath. "Mr. Burns, please! 'The best-laid plans of mousawoo . . .'"

"I will read you Mr. Burns's poem shortly," Penelope said as she wrapped Cassiopeia in a towel. Penelope knew exactly where to find the hair poultice from Miss Mortimer; she had tucked the packet in the back of her dresser drawer earlier, when she first returned to the nursery. "Right now, I have some shampooing of my own to attend to."

THE TWELFTH CHAPTER

*Penelope must
resort to Plan B.*

EVEN WITH THE BRIGHT MORNING sun streaming in her bedchamber window, Penelope's hair looked dull and drab. "The poultice worked perfectly," she thought as she ran the brush through once more. "Now I seem more like my old self, anyway. It reminds me of my Swanburne days. And if the children notice the change in my hair, I will simply tell them I have turned apples into blackberries!"

Clearly, optimism can be a very fine trait, with the power to turn lemons into lemonade, apples into blackberries, and so forth. But just as a scrumptious tarte Philippe will cause the most dreadful tummy ache if eaten in excess, too much optimism can plunge one into the precarious state of mind known as "optoomuchism."

Alas, it is a slippery slope. True optimism, as Agatha Swanburne defined it, is the habit of expecting happy endings in a way that keeps one cheerfully working to make them come true. But optoomuchism is optimism taken much, much too far. It puts one at real risk of getting carried away, or even going overboard, especially when at sea. Caught in the throes of optoomuchism, people become convinced that nothing can go wrong. They invest their life savings in harebrained schemes, buy trans-Atlantic passage on "unsinkable" ships named *Titanic*, and generally fail to recognize when it is time to try Plan B. (Note that in the expression "Plan B," the letter B does not stand for anything in particular; it merely means that when Plan A falls to pieces and disaster looms, it is wise to have an alternative at the ready.)

Penelope's tumble from the velocipede (prompted, as you recall, by her optoomuchstic belief that she could ride blindly through an intersection while sniffing for elephants) had been a painful lesson, and Penelope had already resolved to keep her optimism within reason from that day forward. But old habits die hard. Despite her good intentions, Penelope could not help being cheerful about the lackluster condition of her hair.

"It is a pity there is no way to tell in advance how much optimism is the correct amount," she thought as she pinned her dull, drab locks into a dull, drab bun. "But I fear such judgments can only be made with the gift of hindsight." In this she was correct. And, like a mail-order snow shovel that gets lost by the post office and finally turns up in July, the gift of hindsight always arrives too late to be of practical use.

Still, the day was off to a promising start. Simon was on his way, and the children had updated their journals with pictures of elephants, orangutans, and some brave attempts to spell "Peloponnesian." Alexander had used his wobbly cursive to address all the picture postcards to "Nutsawaoo, Treetops, Ashton Place." Beowulf had decorated each card with a pen-and-ink drawing of a trireme (which, as you may already know, was the many-oared warship used by the ancient Greeks during the Peloponnesian War), and Cassiopeia had signed them "Love Woo Frum Cass." Now she was bouncing with eagerness to drop them in the post.

All in all, it seemed to Penelope that a modest

amount of optimism could safely be given free rein. "Perhaps things are looking up," she thought as she led the children downstairs to wait for Simon, for it was already nearing eleven o'clock. The children would be safe with her, and once they located Madame Ionesco and learned what Simon had discovered on his bookstore excursions, the mysteries posed by Miss Mortimer and the guidebook would doubtless be solved before teatime. The children would find it all highly educational, and Penelope had the pleasant company of Mr. Harley-Dickinson to look forward to.

Truly, what could go wrong?

First, Simon did not show up.

Eleven o'clock came and went. Then eleven-thirty. Then noon. The children grew restless and began to whimper.

It is not easy to wait patiently for someone who is late. In fact, there are many who would grow deeply angry. They would spend the time preparing themselves to boldly confront the tardy person and "read them the riot act," an expression that means to scold someone so thoroughly that he or she will feel as if they have been sprayed full blast with a fire hose.

But Penelope had put her trust in Simon, and her

faith in people was not so easily swayed. First, she waited. Then, she worried. Then, she had what is nowadays called a brainstorm.

"Contraband!" she shouted abruptly, much to the surprise of the Incorrigibles, who had decided to occupy themselves by building a model of a trireme out of bits of the potted fern that sat in the entry foyer. It was Alexander's idea, and a clever one, too, for the fern fronds served nicely as the three tiers of oars that jutted from each side of the ship.

"Contrahwoo?" Beowulf asked, looking up from his work. Penelope paced the slippery floor in deep concentration, for her powers of deduction were at full throttle.

"Contraband means goods which have been illegally obtained," she paused to explain (she was still their governess, after all). "It is the stolen velocipede that has waylaid Mr. Harley-Dickinson, I am certain of it. He must have been stopped by a police officer, for why else would he not be here as planned?"

Thrilled at this dramatic turn of events, the children took up the cry. "Contraband! Contraband!" they whooped. Mrs. Clarke had been upstairs looking for something, but now she waddled down to see what all the ruckus was about.

"Now, now, dearies, don't tell me you're playing at minotaurs again! I thought we learned our lesson about that—"

"Not minotaur, matador—never mind—Mrs. Clarke!" Penelope seized the housekeeper by both arms. "Our friend Mr. Harley-Dickinson may have been thrown in 'the lockup' for being in possession of stolen property. We must help him!"

Mrs. Clarke clucked and shook her head. "You shouldn't get mixed up with that sort, Miss Lumley, that's a bad business all around. Although just hearing the words 'stolen property' put me in mind of old Mr. Clarke, rest his soul." She placed a hand over her heart, and a wave of nostalgia softened her features. "They tossed him in the chokey once a week, in his prime. Disorderly in public was practically his middle name."

Penelope would have very much liked to hear more about the obviously fascinating, dearly departed Mr. Clarke, but she suspected the tale might not be suitable for children's ears, and in any case she was in a hurry. "I assure you, Mrs. Clarke, if any charge has been made, it is a false one. And it will be up to us to prove his innocence. But how?"

She concentrated once more. "I know! Lord Fredrick has a friend, Judge Quinzy, whom I am sure can sort things out, for Simon was in his company all day yesterday. Surely there is no better alibi than the word of a judge! Where might we find him?"

"His Honor? He's a strange duck, isn't he? Gives me gooseflesh to think of him, somehow." Mrs. Clarke gave a little shiver, to demonstrate. "You'll find Judge Quinzy at Lord Fredrick's club, I know it for a fact. The gentlemen had plans to meet for lunch and a game of billiards."

"Do you happen to know the address?" Penelope asked, for after her painful lesson of the previous day, she knew it would be optoomuchstic to try to find Lord Fredrick's club by, say, following the smell of expensive cigars.

"Do I know the address! Who do you think's been sending over Lord Fredrick's clean shirts, shaving kits, new spectacles, skin creams, headache lozenges, and whatever else His Lordship demands? In fact, I was just about to have Old Timothy ride over with this." She waved the book she was holding. "Lord Fredrick's almanac. He wants it, and he wants it right away. You'd think the great Lord Ashton was a sailor, the way he refers to his almanac all day long," Mrs. Clarke said with a sigh. "He checks the moon and the tides the way other men check the financial pages.

But to each his own, I suppose."

"The children and I will bring the almanac to Lord Fredrick ourselves." Penelope practically snatched the volume from Mrs. Clarke. "And Timothy need not trouble himself; we shall take the omnibus." She turned to the Incorrigibles. "Thank you for your patience while waiting, children—and the trireme is very impressive, I must say! But put it aside for now, for at last it is time to go."

"Theatrical haunts with Simawoo?" Cassiopeia asked, confused.

"That was Plan A. Now we are switching to Plan B," Penelope explained. "Perhaps if we can find Simon in prison and obtain his freedom, we can resume Plan A after lunch. Button your coats, please."

"Don't lose that almanac," Mrs. Clarke cautioned, "or Lord Fredrick'll have my head."

"We go to prison?" Alexander asked nervously.

"Guillotine?" Beowulf added, no doubt because of Mrs. Clarke's comment about Lord Fredrick having her head.

"Simawoo no prison!" Cassiopeia insisted. "He perfectly nice!"

Penelope pinned her hat firmly to her dark, dull hair (it was still her old hat, for with all the excitement she had not yet had time to shop for a new one). "You are quite right, Cassiopeia. And, dear me, nobody is going to the guillotine! Come along, everyone. We must speak to Judge Quinzy."

AT THE SWANBURNE ACADEMY FOR Poor Bright Females, all of the girls were taught to have excellent manners, and Penelope was no exception. She knew perfectly well that there was something not quite right about examining another person's property without permission. And yet, as she rode the omnibus with the three Incorrigible children seated next to her and Lord Fredrick's precious almanac in her lap, she found herself deeply curious about the contents of this book. She longed to peek inside the covers, and was finding it difficult to resist doing so.

The children were also interested in the almanac, and peppered her with questions.

"What is almanac?"

"Why a sailor?"

"Why have Mrs. Clarke's head?" Beowulf made a throat-cutting gesture that was so impressively gruesome, it made his sister squeal with delight.

Before answering, Penelope glanced at the address Mrs. Clarke had written down for her, and craned her head out the window to see where they were. "Three more stops, children. Very well. An almanac is like a detailed calendar in book form that includes many facts about nature. It is the sort of information that a farmer—or a sailor—might find useful," she explained. "For example, the almanac will predict when the last frost will come and the ground will be ready for planting, when to expect a dry spell or a rainy one, times of sunrise and sunset, ocean tides, phases of the moon, and so on."

"Moon," Cassiopeia said approvingly. The children were very fond of moons, though a full one did tend to get them worked up.

"Yes, moon." Penelope's desire to teach got the better of her. Impulsively, she flipped open the almanac to the appropriate diagram. "Here, I will show you. These are the phases of the moon—new, crescent, quarter, gibbous, and full—see how it waxes and wanes? And here are all the dates for the year, and . . . hmm, this is odd." For Lord Fredrick, or someone, had circled every single date that there would be a full moon, for the whole year.

The children tried to count the circles, until they made themselves dissolve into laughter and had to start over again: "moon, moon, moon, moon, moon . . ." But it kept them occupied until the omnibus neared their destination.

"Why should Lord Fredrick be so concerned about the full moon?" Penelope wondered. "Perhaps it has to do with his hunting habit, for those would be the brightest nights to go out to the forest—time to stand up, children! This is our stop."

They alighted directly in front of the address Mrs. Clarke had provided. In terms of grandeur the building fell someplace between the London General Post Office and Buckingham Palace, which is to say it was very grand indeed. A burly doorman stood watch at the entrance; happily, his uniform did not include a single tuft of fur. When Penelope and the children approached, he scowled.

"State your business."

"I have something to deliver to Lord Fredrick Ashton." Penelope tried to peer around the doorman but could see nothing; the big fellow loomed too large. "Is he inside?"

"I'll take it to him, miss." The doorman held out his beefy hand.

Instinctively she hugged the almanac close. "Thank you, but I have instructions to hand the item to him personally. It is an object of particular importance to Lord Ashton."

"Moon, moon, moon, moon, moon," Cassiopeia

explained helpfully. Her brothers nodded.

The doorman gave them a curious look. "No offense, but this is the Fox and Hounds Club. It's a gentlemen's club. It's no place for women and children."

Penelope thought of Simon. In her mind's eye she saw him locked in a dungeon somewhere. She stood straight as a poker and spoke in her most no-nonsense voice. "I am Lord Ashton's employee. He requested this volume be brought to him at once, and that is what I intend to do. And these children are his legal wards," she added, though she was not sure how often Lord Fredrick recalled that the Incorrigibles even existed.

The doorman looked the children over. Alexander and Beowulf bowed, and Cassiopeia curtsied. He frowned.

"Very well. Make it quick, though. Lord Ashton's party is in the billiard room; it's just inside and to the left."

Needless to say, Penelope had never entered a wealthy gentleman's club before. The dark wood paneling, sparkling chandeliers, and patterned carpets were as luxurious as one would find in any fine house, but there was a subtle, masculine difference in the feeling of the place. From distant rooms she heard men's voices, gruff and serious, or ringing out with bold laughter. The air carried the scent of pipe tobacco and imported cigars, mixed with the spice of cologne and the saddle smell of expensive leather.

She turned left, as directed, with the children close behind. Now she heard the sharp *clack-clack* of billiard cues, then the muffled thud as the ball hit the felted rim of the table and ricocheted into the pocket. The door to the billiard room was half open. A group of Lord Fredrick's friends were gathered around the green-topped table, cues in hand. There was the Earl of Maytag and Baron Hoover, both of whom Penelope remembered all too well from the Ashton Place holiday ball. Judge Quinzy did not appear to be with them.

"Who goes there?" Baron Hoover called, turning to the door. "What's this? I'm afraid you have taken a wrong turn, miss, quite a wrong turn indeed." Then he looked again. "Why, it's that governess person, isn't it? And aren't those Ashton's famous wolf children?"

"Good day, Baron Hoover." Now all the gentlemen had stopped playing and were looking at Penelope, their expressions a mix of annoyance and curiosity. "I am sorry to disturb your game. The children and I came to deliver this." She held out the almanac. Lord Fredrick seized it at once.

"My almanac! Blast this thing, I'm always losing it." He patted it and promptly tucked it in his pocket. To the men, he shrugged and joked, "One must stay a step ahead of the weather. Wouldn't do to be caught in the rain without a bumbershoot, what?"

"Pardon me." Penelope spoke quickly, before she lost their attention. "I was told Judge Quinzy would be here. Is he expected?"

"He's here, all right. He just stepped outside for some air," the Earl of Maytag snapped, for it was his turn at billiards and he was impatient to resume playing. "What do you want to bother Quinzy about?"

Penelope willed her voice to sound calm. "I am in need of some legal advice."

"Don't get caught. That's all the legal advice anyone needs." Maytag took his shot and dropped a ball in the side pocket with a neat *click*.

"Har, har! And possession is nine-tenths of the law," added Baron Hoover, relighting his pipe.

"In other words, finders keepers! Speaking of which, what is the condition of those Incorrigible pups these days?" Lord Fredrick squinted in the direction of the children, who huddled in the doorway. "Still howling and whatnot?"

"Pups? Don't be rude, Freddy. At Christmas they were spouting Latin, as I recall. An impressive trick, I must say." Maytag applied chalk to the tip of his cue.

"I am in need of some legal advice."

"Tell us, children, what have you been studying lately?"

The children stepped forward to answer.

"Peloponnesian War," mumbled Alexander.

"Bears," said Beowulf, sounding defiant.

"Moon, moon, moon, moon," Cassiopeia counted. The child opened her mouth in a way that let Penelope know she was about to let out a howl of anxiety; she clapped her hand over the girl's face and said, "We have been enjoying the cultural sights of London. Today we hoped to have a tour of the theater district, but I fear our guide may have been detained by the police. If so, it is all a misunderstanding, for he is a perfectly nice young man. That is why I wish to speak to His Honor."

"Surely you do not mean Mr. Harley-Dickinson?" Judge Quinzy entered the room in three long strides, bearing a snifter of some dark, syrupy liquid. "Is our young playwright in trouble with the law? I am disappointed to hear it. He hardly seemed the type."

"The theater attracts all sorts of shady characters. Always has," Baron Hoover observed.

Alexander nodded. "Aristophanes."

"Gesundheit." Baron Hoover replied, waving his pipe in the other direction. "Sorry about the smoke; I'll ring for someone to open a window."

Alexander was about to explain that Aristophanes

was the famous Greek dramatist who wrote satirical plays about the Peloponnesian War, but Penelope spoke first. "As I said, it is a misunderstanding. Do you remember the velocipede I was riding yesterday?"

Judge Quinzy settled himself in a leather club chair and swirled his drink. "It would be hard to forget," he said wryly, "seeing as how you crashed it into my carriage."

"I am sorry about that." Penelope hoped no one noticed her blush. "Mr. Harley-Dickinson used the velocipede to run an errand, but there is a chance it may be stolen property, and now I fear he is being held by the authorities."

"Why do you think that?"

"Because he did not show up for our appointment this morning."

"And it did not occur to you that he may have simply found something better to do?"

"No, sir. It did not."

"I see." Judge Quinzy looked vaguely amused. "Miss Lumley, I am afraid that legal problems are never as simple as they may first appear. Before I render a verdict, let me consult my colleagues." He addressed the men at the billiards table. "What say you, gentlemen? A man is found riding a velocipede that turns out to be stolen, but he claims he is not the thief. Opinions?"

The Earl of Maytag did not hesitate. "Caught with stolen property? Hang him! No honest man scoots around on pilfered wheels. He's obviously guilty of something."

Lord Ashton shook his head in disagreement. "Finders keepers, I say. A velocipede belongs to the person who's riding it. Case closed, what?"

Baron Hoover paused to take a shot, which missed, and straightened from the table with a grunt. "Now, Freddy, that's a bit unfeeling, isn't it? What about the poor chap who owned the velocipede to begin with? Doesn't he deserve some justice? Chances are he left it outside a shop and someone rode off on it. Or maybe the 'thief' thought it was abandoned and free for the taking. Could've been an honest mistake. I say more investigation is required."

Judge Quinzy leaned back in his chair and steepled his fingers. "You see how difficult the work of a judge is, Miss Lumley? Three men, three different opinions."

Penelope was flummoxed; to her the situation had seemed quite straightforward, until now. And why had Maytag found it necessary to mention hanging in front of the children? "Your Honor, Mr. Harley-Dickinson was with you yesterday, at the zoo. Surely you would be able to explain to the police that he could not have done anything wrong?"

Judge Quinzy shook his head. "Unless we know exactly what time the property was stolen, and from what address, an alibi is irrelevant."

"But what if we found the true owner of the velocipede, and returned it? Wouldn't that solve everything?"

"In a city the size of London?" Judge Quinzy smiled. "It would be no more possible to determine the rightful owner of that velocipede than it would be to determine the origins of those three remarkable pupils of yours."

"Respectfully, I disagree." Her fear made Penelope bold. "For how can one say something is impossible, if one has not tried?"

For a tense moment, it was as if Penelope and Judge Quinzy were the only two people in the room.

"Have you tried to discover their origins, then? Do tell us what you have learned," he murmured.

"You mean, the children's?" she blurted. "Why, no. I was talking about the velocipede . . ."

"A far more interesting topic, I quite agree," the Earl of Maytag interjected. "First we must determine: Was the velocipede lost, abandoned, or stolen? In my view it makes all the difference. For if it was lost or abandoned, then I agree with Ashton. Finders keepers."

"Hear, hear," Lord Ashton said absently; he was busy thumbing through the almanac.

"But if stolen—hanging's too good for him. Unless Miss Lumley can point us in the direction of the real thief, of course."

Penelope thought of the little urchin boy. Perhaps he had stolen the velocipede—she had assumed as much—but she could not know for certain, could she? And with all this talk of hanging, how could she dream of accusing a poor waif of a child, who likely had no one to teach him right from wrong to begin with?

Or perhaps Judge Quinzy was right. Perhaps Simon had simply found something better to do this morning. Even as she considered this, she did not believe it. Call her optoomuchstic, but she did not think Simon would have broken his word.

"So which is it, Miss Lumley?" Judge Quinzy held out his hands. "Lost, abandoned, or stolen?"

"I cannot say for certain where the velocipede came from, Your Honor," she replied. "I am sorry. I see now that I should not have troubled you with this matter."

He nodded, as if he had known that would be her conclusion all along.

Baron Hoover chuckled. "My advice is to not get

tangled up with the law to begin with. Once you do, it's a sticky wicket, that's for sure! Not easy to extricate oneself, har har."

"Spiderweb," Beowulf observed, but Alexander shushed him gently.

"Should you ever see Mr. Harley-Dickinson again," the judge said smoothly, "do tell him I wish him all the best, and trust this incident will serve as a valuable lesson. By the way, are you feeling well, Miss Lumley?" He paused. "Your complexion seems rather pale today. I hope you are not coming down with a cold."

Penelope adjusted her hat to cover as much of her hair as possible, for she knew the dark hair made her face look sallow by comparison. "I am quite well, I assure you. Good day."

Desperate to leave, she turned and shepherded the children toward the door. But as she did, Judge Quinzy's words rang in her head.

. . . those three remarkable pupils . . .

Have you tried to discover their origins?

Lost, abandoned, or stolen? . . . Lost, abandoned, or stolen?

Could the Incorrigibles have been stolen? Not lost in the woods while being neglected by the world's most careless parents, or abandoned there by the world's most cruel and unfeeling parents, but actually *stolen* from what must surely be the world's most worried and heartbroken parents?

It was such an awful thought she could not prevent herself from exclaiming, "Oh, my!"

Baron Hoover was on his feet. "What is it, my dear?"

If Penelope were to answer honestly, she would say, "I just realized that I had formed a poor opinion of two people whom I have never met, and now I wish to apologize but cannot, because I don't know who they are."

But instead, she blurted, "I just remembered that the children have not yet taken their naps. We must be on our way. Good day."

At this, the Incorrigibles began to protest.

"Not sleepy, Lumawoo!"

"Awake awake awake-*ahwoo*!"

"No nap! Mew-eezum!" begged Cassiopeia.

"We will discuss it outside, children. This way, please." As she hurried them out of the billiard room, the door ever so slowly closed behind them. As it did, she overheard:

"Those wolf-children of yours are positively mad." It was the Earl of Maytag's voice. "Can't imagine why you bother with them, Freddy. They must be a dreadful expense to feed. And the noise! All that barking and yapping and *ahwoo*ing. Why not give them to the zoo?"

"Finders keepers!" Lord Fredrick crowed. "Let's play more billiards, shall we?"

"GIVE THE CHILDREN TO THE ZOO!" Penelope fumed. What sort of people were they, who could talk in such a callous way? And was it truly possible that the Incorrigibles themselves might be, in a sense, contraband?

It was a spiderweb indeed, and Penelope felt as if she were trapped in one of those frightening dreams that everyone has now and then, in which a miniature Penelope was pinned to the sticky middle of the web, with a giant, black-robed arachnid bearing Judge Quinzy's face scuttling ever nearer. It was an unpleasant image, to say the least, and she quickly dispelled it by concentrating on her surroundings.

The only other people waiting for the omnibus were a mother with two babies in one of the new wheeled perambulators that could be pushed from behind. The babies were at the age when they could sit up quite well and enjoy the scenery. They were dressed alike and appeared to be twins; their mother entertained them with a variety of rattles, plush toys, nursery rhymes, games of peek-a-boo, and amusing little songs about farm animals. The babies laughed and clapped their chubby hands, while the Incorrigibles watched, mesmerized.

Penelope found it a fascinating scene as well—what a clever idea, making a miniature carriage to push babies in!—but soon realized that it was the mother's loving, singsong attentions that had so thoroughly captured the Incorrigibles' attention, just as it had the babies'.

"Never fear, somehow we will figure out who your parents are," she so dearly wanted to tell them. But she did not, for she would hate to make such a promise and not be able to keep it. Penelope had the unshakable confidence of a Swanburne girl about most things, but when it came to finding missing parents—well, put it this way: She had not had much luck with it in her own life, so far.

And, frankly, since she still needed to rescue Simon and sort out the business of the stolen velocipede, the mystery of the peculiar guidebook, and the case of the missing soothsayer, it seemed best to postpone tackling any further mysteries for the time being. "One conundrum at a time," she concluded, "and none on an empty stomach." Or, in the words of Agatha Swanburne: "First, eat."

At last the omnibus arrived. Alexander and Beowulf

were delighted to hold the two babies as Penelope helped the woman lift her carriage aboard. During the ride Cassiopeia entertained the infants with her own doggy-themed version of the farm animal song, in which every animal either barked or howled. The babies found it hilarious.

Penelope watched this odd yet adorable scene unfold. "Sooner or later, we *will* find out who your parents are. I will make sure of it," she thought. But aloud she said only, "One more stop until Muffinshire Lane. Alexander, would you please ring the bell?"

THE THIRTEENTH CHAPTER

*Lady Constance has one
epiphany after another.*

THE PELOPONNESIAN WAR LASTED FOR twenty-seven years, which would be considered a long time nowadays. Rest assured, it was a long time in ancient Greece, too. One might wonder why the Athenians and the Spartans did not sit down over a nice cup of tea and work out their differences, but they did not. Instead, they fought long and hard over questions like which of them had the most naval strength and the superior form of government. There was a six-year peace in the middle (rather like the intermission of a play), but then the fighting started up all over again. It must have been very tedious for all concerned.

Wars, it cannot be said too often, are a dreadful business, and this one was surely no different. But just as optimism has its dark side, the Peloponnesian War was not without its bright spots, at least in terms of literature. It prompted an Athenian general named Thucydides to write a gripping work of history called *The History of the Peloponnesian War* and (as Alexander observed to Baron Hoover) a clever playwright named Aristophanes to write comic plays that made fun of the generals, including, one supposes, Thucydides.

Now, unless one has been told by one's governess to write an essay on the subject, the causes and consequences of a war that has been over for thousands of years is unlikely to be a topic of dinner table conversation. Yet Thucydides's history and Aristophanes's plays are still enjoyed to this very day, which proves that, when it comes to liking a good story, people have not changed very much at all.

However, the Incorrigibles' governess *had* told them to write about the causes and consequences of the Peloponnesian War, so it was all quite fresh in their minds. After lunch they debated the relevant issues with gusto.

"Navy!"

"Trade!"

"Helots!" Helots were what the Spartans called their slaves.

"Democracy versus oligarchy," Alexander pronounced with confidence.

"Plague-*ahwoo*," his sister observed. For it was an outbreak of plague that finally did the Athenians in and forced them to surrender to the Spartans. To make her point clear, Cassiopeia mimed dying a gruesome death from plague; it was marvelously convincing. If done in public, it would no doubt assure anyone of getting a seat on even the most crowded omnibus.

"Plague-ahwoo, that is correct," Penelope mumbled distractedly, for she was busy thumbing through a stack of books, searching for some clue as to how to rescue Simon. Where were prisoners kept in this vast, unfeeling city? And how did one secure their escape? A fuller understanding of the workings of the legal system was what she needed, but without access to a law library she had only the stack of novels she had brought from Ashton Place as a reference. Within these books she found tales of bloody revolutions and innocent men falsely accused, all of which seemed to end with nooses and guillotines. As plots went, they were thrilling, but the thought of Simon in such a predicament filled Penelope with dread.

"Dear me! A rollicking story is a marvelous thing, but these are far more exciting than one would ever wish real life to be," she told herself. "I had best put my books away and consult Mrs. Clarke about the matter. She seemed to have personal experience of bailing someone out of prison. I hope it will not stir painful memories if I ask her advice."

"Plague-*ahwoooo*!" Cassiopeia howled mournfully as she choked and gasped on the floor.

At that inconvenient moment, Lady Constance burst into the nursery. "Miss Lumley, what an extraordinary adventure I have had!" she announced. "So extraordinary that I simply must tell someone about it, even if it is only you, and even if I had to walk up several flights of stairs to do it." She paused for dramatic effect. "Miss Lumley, I believe I am having an epiphany!"

An "epiphany," in case you have yet to have one, is when someone encounters truths about life with which they were previously unfamiliar, thus sparking an abrupt change of perspective. If the change is unpleasant, it is "a rude awakening." If enlightening, it is called "having an epiphany." Neither experience is medically dangerous, though the person in question may find themselves mulling things over for a good while afterward.

"I said, an epiphany!" Lady Constance repeated, now sounding a bit cross. "Don't you want to know about what?"

"Of course, my lady." Her mistress's arrival was unexpected, to say the least, and Penelope found herself flustered and wishing she had put away her recently laundered stockings, which were hung to dry by the window. Also, Cassiopeia was still rolling on the ground, twitching and foaming at the mouth quite brilliantly.

"I am having an epiphany about the poor," Lady Constance proclaimed, stepping daintily over the writhing child. "Believe it or not, I have spent the day among paupers. A pauper is someone who is *exceptionally* poor," she added, by way of explanation to Alexander and Beowulf. They stared at her with fascination, largely because the decorations on her hat included a small stuffed bird. "Not an ordinary poor person, mind you, but someone who has *excelled* at being destitute."

At that, Cassiopeia's eyes rolled back in her head. After a few final death throes, she went limp. The stellar performance briefly distracted the boys' eyes from the bird, and they politely applauded.

Oblivious, Lady Constance flounced around the tiny room. She put her frilly purse on the bedside table and examined herself in the mirror. "You know, Miss Lumley, one occasionally hears talk about poor people, but all the conversation in the world does nothing to prepare one for the absolute *shock* of meeting them in the flesh. I hope it is not unladylike for me to say so, but the paupers Baroness Hoover and I visited were filthy to the point of disgrace." Lady Constance turned and fanned herself. "And their apartments! They were so tiny and depressing! Why they choose to live there is beyond me."

"It is puzzling, yes," Penelope murmured, keeping close watch on the boys, whose eyes were again fixed on the bouncing bird. Beowulf had begun to drool, which was never a good sign.

"I told them in the sternest possible terms that they must stop dithering away the hours in those dreadful factories they insist on going to every day, and devote their time to worthier pursuits. Like interior decorating! I am no seamstress, of course, but honestly, how hard could it be to fashion a pretty tablecloth out of some lace? It would lend a touch of badly needed charm to all that squalor. Where on earth is the bellpull?"

"I believe it is by the door, Lady Constance," Penelope replied, although she was unsure, as she was not in the habit of ringing for servants.

Lady Constance searched and yanked vigorously on a cord, which turned out to be the tieback for the drapes. On her next try she got it right, and the bell echoed anxiously through the house.

She turned back to the mirror and poked at the poor little bird, which had fallen askew. "Here is something else I learned about the poor, Miss Lumley: They do not even bother to dress for dinner. It is really quite appalling. Margaret!" she screeched impatiently.

"Here I am, m'lady!" The pretty young housemaid finally appeared, with her high voice squeaky as a fiddle and her cheeks flushed from running up the stairs double time. "I didn't expect you'd be in the nursery, my lady. It's lovely that you take a maternal interest in the children, I must say. . . ." Margaret looked down in alarm. Cassiopeia was still frozen on the floor in plague position, like an actor at the end of tragic play after all the principal characters have killed one another and the last surviving cast member must deliver a stirring monologue summing up what it all means, while his fellow actors lie there covered with fake blood, trying not to giggle.

Lady Constance stepped over Cassiopeia again. "I wish you wouldn't dawdle so, Margaret! I have been standing here for the better part of a minute. Now draw me a bath, please, and lay out a fresh gown." Lady Constance sniffed the air. "I have been in the most malodorous surroundings imaginable and feel the need to be thoroughly scrubbed."

"At once, my lady." Margaret curtsied and started to dash out to obey, but her kind heart got the better of her. "Is the little girl all right, Miss Lumley?"

Penelope started to tell Margaret how the Athenians lost the Peloponnesian War, but Alexander beat her to the punch.

"Plague," the boy explained. "Bubonic."

"Black death," Beowulf added.

Cassiopeia opened one eye and coughed pathetically. "Plague-*ahwoooooooooo*!" she howled.

Margaret screamed, and a squeaky, piercing, blood-curdling scream it was. Lady Constance screamed as well. "What! No! Heavens! I scarcely survive traipsing through the slums, only to find my own house infected with plague! Eek! Eek!"

"Do not panic!" Penelope cried. "She is only pretending!" The boys yapped in agreement. In the melee, the little bird fell off Lady Constance's hat and disappeared somewhere in the nursery. Finally Cassio-peia sat up and smiled, proving she was not, in fact, dead from the plague, and everyone settled down.

"Sorry, Miss Lumley," Margaret said, composing herself. "Didn't mean to shriek like a banshee! I was startled, is all. It was so lifelike! She's a talented lass, isn't she?"

Lady Constance scowled. "Pretending to die of plague! Have you ever heard of such a thing? These children are not quite right, Miss Lumley. Just because my husband has chosen to keep them does not mean they can behave like wild animals in my house."

"I understand, Lady Constance," Penelope began to explain, "but the children have been quite swept up in the military history of ancient Greece, and one thing led to another—"

"Gibberish!" declared Lady Constance, whose own education had consisted largely of advanced studies in shopping, flirting, and hair care.

"I beg your pardon," Alexander said politely. "Your bird." He tapped his brother on the shoulder. Beowulf meekly opened his mouth and extracted the bird. He held it out to Lady Constance.

"Soggy, sorry," he apologized.

Lady Constance backed herself to the door in

horror. "This is *precisely* what I mean! Lord Fredrick will hear about this, I warn you! Margaret, I must have a bath at once! Extra hot!"

AFTER LADY CONSTANCE HAD GONE, the stuffed bird was hung by the window to dry, next to the stockings. Penelope decided that a math lesson was just the thing to restore some calm to the nursery, and soon the Incorrigibles were well on their way to mastering how to figure the area of a triangle. Penelope left them a few practice problems to keep them occupied and then went downstairs to find Mrs. Clarke, to ask her advice about how to spring someone from prison.

But Mrs. Clarke was out. Penelope was surprised to hear it, for Mrs. Clarke ran the household with the iron hand of, well, a Spartan general, and that meant she was nearly always on the premises. Moreover, none of the servants could say where she had gone, or when she might return.

Back up the stairs she trudged. Penelope did not like to admit it, but her store of optimism was fast running out. She had already switched from Plan A to Plan B, but she was not one smidgen closer to rescuing Simon, locating the missing fortune-teller, or cracking the mystery of the *Hixby's Guide*. Now even Plan

C (in this particular case, the C can be made to stand for Consulting Mrs. Clarke) was not working out. Just like the wee mousie in the poem by Mr. Robert Burns, it seemed as if Penelope's best-laid plans were being thwarted at every turn.

Penelope could think of only one other person to turn to for help: her former headmistress, Miss Charlotte Mortimer. "But given our recent conversation I expect she will tell me to be a good governess and not worry," she thought unhappily. "And what secret is she keeping about the *Hixby's Guide*? If it is truly a secret, then she is unlikely to tell me, but I suppose I can still write to her and ask." She did so, and dropped the letter in the tray to be picked up at the next post.

With an hour yet before teatime, their lessons already completed, and Mrs. Clarke nowhere to be found, there was nothing to do but take the children on an educational outing of some sort. But to where? They were still keen to see the theatrical haunts Simon had promised (they felt this way even after Penelope explained that there would be no actual ghosts involved), so Penelope led the Incorrigibles on a walk through the theater district. The children *oohed* and *aahed* as they strolled past the marquees and the

216

colorful posters advertising the entertainments within, but the sight simply made Penelope fret all the more about the fate of her playwright friend.

"Perhaps he will find interesting ideas for plots among the shady characters he meets in the lockup," she thought, but it left her feeling even sadder that Simon was not with them. As they walked, she wondered which of the theaters was the one where Simon's stage manager acquaintance would have let them in to watch a rehearsal. If not for that stolen velocipede, perhaps they might have gotten a glimpse of:

THE GREAT LEOTARDO, MASTER OF THE TRAPEZE!

Or:

PIRATES ON HOLIDAY: A SEAWORTHY OPERETTA (WORLD PREMIERE)

Or even:

THE TRAGICAL TALE OF KING AETHELRED THE NOT SO GREAT (A MOST INGLORIOUS KING WAS HE)

Each one sounded more thrilling than the last! Particularly the one about the pirates. Penelope's disappointment was excruciating. She considered purchasing tickets herself, but they were expensive, and although Penelope's salary was generous, Lady Constance rarely paid it unless Penelope asked. After that unfortunate mix-up about the plague, Penelope knew that Lady Constance was much too cross with her and the children to approach.

Then Cassiopeia begged to see the British Mew-eezum, but Penelope did not want to take the children anywhere near it until she knew what, if anything, Simon had discovered about the *Hixby's Guide*—what if Gallery Seventeen were a trap of some sort? So instead they visited the Royal Exhibition of Pteridological Rarities, a small but fascinating collection of freak-ish ferns. There they saw ferns with leaves instead of fronds, ferns that loved the sun, ferns that lacked spo-rangia altogether, and other bizarre flukes of nature.

It was all quite educational, of course. But Penelope was still too worried about Simon to take any real plea-sure in it. Given how Penelope felt about ferns, this was a very bad sign indeed.

THINGS WERE NOT LOOKING UP at all. In fact, they were looking decidedly glum—at least for Penelope, they were. But when the seesaw of good fortune sinks downward for one person, it is very often on its way up for someone else. This little-known law of physics is called the Fulcrum of Fortune, and although most peo-ple prefer to think of fortune as a wheel that spins, the fulcrum (that is, seesaw) is a more accurate depiction for most of us, since the worse our own luck becomes, the more likely we are to notice the good fortune of those around us and brood about the injustice of it all.

In Penelope's case, the Fulcrum of Fortune was indisputably at work, for while she and the children were out, the post came, and came, and came yet again. Each delivery brought a fresh torrent of mail to Number Twelve Muffinshire Lane. And despite the fact that Penelope was positively desperate to hear news of Simon or receive some sort of reply from Miss Mortimer, every single letter was addressed to Lady Constance Ashton.

Lady Constance herself could scarcely believe it. She held the envelopes up to the light and turned each one over in her hands several times before she dared open it. But the shock soon wore off, and she began to await each postal delivery with glee. She even insisted that the sacks of mail be weighed on the kitchen scale, so she could brag about how many pounds of letters she had received.

By the day's final post at eight o'clock, so much mail had come that Lady Constance sent for Penelope with the curt message that "the services of an educated person are required" to help open, sort, and reply to the heaping piles of correspondence.

Penelope would have much preferred to stay in the nursery, building triremes out of toothpicks with the children until bedtime, but she could hardly refuse Lady Constance. And she still hoped to speak to Mrs. Clarke, so perhaps it would be just as well to spend the rest of the evening downstairs in the parlor. That way she would know the instant the housekeeper returned from wherever it was she had gone.

"And, too," she thought, "if I prove helpful regarding her mail, it might smooth things over between us. But truly, what an unexpected reversal! Why so many letters, after so few?" Indeed, the abrupt change in Lady Constance's postal fortunes was puzzling, but the answer to the puzzle had already arrived—by post, of course.

"This is curious," Lady Constance commented as she opened a long, official-looking envelope. "It is from the postmaster, London General Post Office, London. I hope they are not demanding payment for the extra volume of mail, tee hee!"

Two golden eyebrows furrowed into one as Lady Constance digested the contents of the letter. After a moment the paper slipped from her grasp. "Miss Lumley! We are at Number Twelve Muffinshire Lane!" she exclaimed in a tone of utter surprise.

Penelope was well aware of her location—particularly after all those navigational studies with the children—but to Lady Constance the news seemed to have the makings of yet another epiphany. "I told all my acquaintances that we were staying at Number Twelve *Biscuitshire* Lane," she went on, amazed. "So all the mail intended for me was held up at the post office, for as it happens, there is no Biscuitshire Lane in London! The postmaster himself has written to apologize for the delay!"

Lady Constance rose and fairly danced around the parlor. "I knew it! My friends had not forgotten me after all. And how clever the post office is to realize I meant Muffin, not Biscuit! Such a display of competence is almost enough to make one not mind paying the postal tax, although you must *never* tell Fredrick I said so."

Overcome with joy, she tossed armfuls of mail into the air until the room was buried in a blizzard of paper, thus undoing Penelope's efforts to keep everything in order. "Look at all these invitations! Luncheons! Dinners! Weekends! Drives through the park! Games of croquet! How I love London. I am *so* glad I thought of coming here! And look, here is the very best invitation of all."

"How I love London. I am so glad
I thought of coming here!"

She brandished another, smaller envelope. "It is a gift from Baroness Hoover, in appreciation for all I have done for the poor and downtrodden." She paused to wipe away a pretend tear, and then resumed her boasting. "It says that Fredrick and I are invited to the world premiere of a comic operetta called *Pirates on Holiday*. Baroness Hoover says it has been sold out for weeks, and yet we are going, how clever she must be to get tickets! Of course, I am not at all sure about pirates; it has a kind of criminal feel to it, frankly—but I suppose it will be entertaining, in a popular sort of way."

Pirates on Holiday! Penelope's bitterness about the recent collapse of her own fortunes grew tenfold. Oh, the injustice of it all! And where, oh, where was Simon?

Lady Constance returned to her seat and fixed Penelope with a bright, almost manic stare. "Miss Lumley! Since you are our resident scholar, allow me to ask you a question: What sort of jewelry does one wear to the theater? Are pearls too stuffy? Would emeralds be gauche? If it were the symphony, the answer would be simple: diamonds, diamonds, and more diamonds!" Lady Constance looked at her expectantly.

"I—I cannot say, my lady," Penelope stammered. "I know little about jewelry, for I do not own any."

Lady Constance scowled. "Tut tut, of course you do

not. I simply thought that as a matter of cultural information, you might know what goes on in theaters. But I suppose they did not have time to cover such topics in your Swanbird education, what with all your studies of plague and whatnot."

"Swanburne." Penelope knew the name was unlikely to stick in Lady Constance's mind, but she was feeling so gloomy she simply could not stand it anymore. "I attended the Swanburne Academy for Poor Bright Females."

"Swanburne, Swanburne, of course! Why is that so hard to remember?" Obviously Lady Constance could hardly expect Penelope to have an answer to this question, but she asked it nevertheless. "Swanburne Academy, Poor Bright Females. Swanburne Academy, Poor Bright Females. *Oh!* My!" She shrieked as if she had been pinched. "Miss Lumley, does that mean you yourself were once poor?"

Penelope squirmed and wondered if she were about to be fired. "I suppose it does," she replied carefully, "or else they would not have accepted me."

Lady Constance rose and looked Penelope squarely in the eye.

"Miss Lumley, this is shocking news. Earlier, I said many unpleasant things about the poor. At the time, I had no idea that you had ever had anything to do with such people, or might even be counted among them. Now I feel I ought to apologize."

Then Lady Constance marched briskly out of the parlor, calling loudly for Margaret so that she might plan her outfit for the opening of *Pirates on Holiday*. Penelope was left to finish opening and sorting the mail herself.

"Feeling one ought to apologize is not quite the same thing as saying 'I am sorry,'" she thought sadly as she poked her letter opener into the next envelope in the pile. "But where Lady Constance Ashton is concerned, I suppose one could call it progress."

It was the most optimistic thought she had had all day.

THE FOURTEENTH CHAPTER

Lord Fredrick comes down
with a head cold, of sorts.

IT WAS NOT UNTIL THE next morning that Penelope finally discovered the reason for Mrs. Clarke's absence. Apparently the dear old housekeeper had had a bit of an epiphany herself; in fact, she was so eager to talk about it that she launched into her tale before Penelope could ask her advice about Simon. Now the story was under way, and all Penelope could do was listen and wait for some kind of opening to present itself.

"It was because of you, Miss Lumley, and the way you got me remembering old Mr. Clarke," Mrs. Clarke confided over an early morning cup of tea in the nursery, while the children ate their breakfasts nearby. "It struck me that I hadn't been to see his gravesite in many a year, though I couldn't tell you why; I just never got around to it, I suppose. And that got me feeling all—not teary eyed, exactly, but in that quiet sort of thinking mood where you sit and wonder why things are the way they are. What's the word?"

"Philosophical?" Penelope suggested.

Mrs. Clarke snorted. "No, nothing so grand as that! But I couldn't stop marveling at how fast the time goes, and how complicated life is, but how simple, too, and how most people don't appreciate the minutes ticking by until they're gone, gone, gone. That sort of thing. Pass the scones, would you, dear?"

Penelope obliged, and took another for herself, too. "Agatha Swanburne once said something in that vein," she commented. "She said, 'You're not where you were, and you're not where you're going. You're here, so pay attention!'" Although nothing could compare to tarte Philippe, the scones were quite good, Penelope had to admit.

"Pay attention, eh?" Mrs. Clarke spread a fat dollop of clotted cream on her scone. "I'd like to meet your friend Agatha sometime. She sounds like a clever girl."

Agatha Swanburne was long dead, of course, although she had lived to be a very elderly person indeed. But Mrs. Clarke's words made Penelope realize that she did not know where the wise old woman was buried. Nor had she ever stopped to wonder if anyone was in the habit of visiting the gravesite, and perhaps leaving flowers.

"Does Agatha Swanburne have any surviving relatives?" Penelope wondered. "I certainly do not know of any." Unlike, say, Lord Fredrick's study at Ashton Place, which showcased the whole parade of Ashton forbears in a series of oil paintings so dark and brooding that, if they had been Landscapes, they certainly would be considered Ominous, at the Swanburne Academy the portrait of Agatha Swanburne was displayed all alone. It hung in a place of honor in the headmistress's office, where the founder's wise yet impish face gazed down at any student who happened to end up sitting across from Miss Mortimer's desk.

"How strange, that the Swanburne family tree is not better known. Surely there are many proud and loyal Swanburne girls who would be curious about it." These and other interesting thoughts could easily have occupied her for another scone or two, yet Penelope shook them off, for she realized she had stopped paying attention altogether, and Mrs. Clarke was still talking.

"You know I hardly ever have a day off, not even on my birthday! But I thought to myself, Nellie"—until that moment Penelope had had no idea that Mrs. Clarke's first name was Nellie—"Nellie, old girl, it's high time you took a day, just for yourself. Buy a new hat and have a stroll in the park. If Lady Constance has a conniption fit, that's her problem. It wouldn't be the first time, and it won't be the last. So that's what I did. Mr. Clarke's buried out in the countryside, so I couldn't visit his grave, poor dear, but in his honor I walked the cemetery in Kensal Green and thought of times gone by. It's a lovely place, and the walk did my poor heart good. On the way back I found a confectioner's shop, too. I bought some sweeties for the children—they do eat sweeties, don't they?"

As Mrs. Clarke well knew, the children could be fussy about meat dishes (which they preferred cooked quite rare and slathered with ketchup), but when it came to candy—well, what child does not like candy?

Before answering, Penelope glanced at the Incorrigibles. They had finished breakfast; she noted with pride that they had cleared their own bowls and taken out their journals without being asked. "I am sure the children will be delighted. And speaking of Mr. Clarke," she went on, seizing the chance to change the subject, "based on your experience, is there some way to find out for certain if my acquaintance Mr. Harley-Dickinson is in police custody, and if he is, how to 'spring him,' as it were?"

Mrs. Clarke chuckled. "Still thinking about that young fella, eh? Miss Lumley, my advice is to leave him where he is until he's slept off whatever potent refreshment landed him in the lockup to begin with. If he's anything like Mr. Clarke, he'll be ever so sorry and meek as a lamb when he gets out. Maybe it'll teach him a lesson. Not that being sorry ever made Mr. Clarke change his ways!"

She laughed, deep and hearty. "Oh, how I used to scold! Makes me blush to think of the things I said. And now the poor man's buried in the ground, and I won't be scolding him again, that's for sure." Still laughing, she dabbed away a tear with her napkin. "'Pay attention,' is that what your friend Agatha said? It's as good advice as any. I hope I can follow it."

ALTHOUGH SHE DID NOT SEE it that way, Mrs. Clarke's change of perspective was both philosophical in nature and genuinely enlightening, and thus could be considered a true epiphany. On the other hand, Lady Constance's shock and distaste at meeting people less fortunate than her pampered self had the potential to be a rude awakening—that is, if the lady had shown any signs of waking up.

So far she had not. In Lady Constance's mind, those hard-to-get tickets to *Pirates on Holiday* were a well-deserved payment for her own kindness and charitable spirit. Now that she had her reward in hand, the problem of what to do about the poor was, in her opinion, as solved as it needed to be.

"It is a marvelous thing, knowing that one has done one's bit for the less fortunate," she proclaimed as Margaret pulled, pinned, yanked, and braided her yellow locks into submission. "But I will not be repeating the experience anytime soon. I should never be able to stand the smell!"

Lady Constance was in high spirits, and why not? She and Lord Fredrick would have an early dinner at an expensive restaurant (but not at the Fern Court; even the well-connected Baroness Hoover had been unable to get reservations at the Piazza Hotel on such short notice), followed by an open-air carriage ride through the park, and then on to the premiere of *Pirates on Holiday*. The question of what the lady ought to wear to the theater had been settled with a touch of whimsy: After much deliberation, she had instructed Margaret to whip up a bejeweled satin eye patch and a belted scabbard made of felt and rhinestones, which she planned to wear slung around the skirt of her seaweed green gown.

"I know it is a theatrical premiere and not a fancy-dress ball," she said as she waited for the rhinestones to be sewn on, "but really, who could object? It is festive, and being festive keeps things cheerful, don't you agree, Margaret?"

"I wouldn't disagree, my lady," Margaret replied diplomatically, for who would dare contradict Lady Constance?

Penelope was sorry to have to be privy to this conversation, but alas, the idea that she could be used as a personal secretary had taken root in Lady Constance's mind. She had summoned Penelope four times since luncheon, so that she might dictate replies to her correspondence. But the lady had endless trouble deciding what to say; she kept starting and stopping and rewording what Penelope had already written down, until page after page was ruined and had to be copied afresh.

Then Lady Constance lost interest altogether, and

Penelope ended up writing most of the letters herself. She amused herself by signing each one with a different socially useful phrase, of the type the children were so adept at. "Yours in solidarity, Lady A." "With most gracious wishes for your continued recovery, Lady A." "With fondest thoughts on this, the day of your birth, Lady A." And so on.

At last the eye patch was finished, and Margaret adjusted it carefully so as not to muss Lady Constance's elaborately upswept hair. Lady Constance shrieked with delight when she finally opened her remaining eye and admired herself in the mirror. "Mark my words," she crowed, "once I am seen wearing this, the decorative eye patch will be all the rage. By the weekend, fashionable young ladies all over London will be swaggering about like sailors. Imagine, a lady pirate! What an original idea, and it is all mine!"

"Actually, there have been many famous lady pirates," Penelope felt compelled to say. "Anne Bonny, Lady Killigrew, Grace O'Malley—to name only a few."

Slowly, Lady Constance turned. Even with one eye, she still managed to glower with displeasure.

"Miss Lumley, my father used to say that too much education made a girl tedious. I am beginning to see his point." Then she turned to the nimble-fingered maid. "Margaret, I am curious. Are your parents poor, too? Like Miss Lumley's?"

Penelope did not know whether to feel shamed or angered by Lady Constance's remark. Margaret threw her a puzzled glance before answering. "I wouldn't say so, my lady. It's never easy to get by, but Mum takes in extra washing and my brother, Frank, helps Pa in the smithy. Ever since a horse spooked and kicked him in the knee, Pa's been awful lame. But Frank can shoe a horse as fast as any man in the county, and he's just a lad of twelve."

"Good, honest labor," Lady Constance said approvingly as she gazed into her vanity mirror. "I am glad to hear it. For how could Lord Ashton and I take a pleasant turn in a carriage of a Sunday, if our horses were not properly shod—eek! Is that a pimple?"

"Ahwoooooooo!"

"Woof! Woof!"

"Ahwoooooooo!"

From somewhere inside the house it came: the unmistakable sound of howling and barking. Penelope blanched. "If you will forgive me, Lady Constance, I ought not to leave the children unattended for so long—"

"Ahwoooooooo!"

"Woof! Woof!"

"Ahwooooooooo!"

The noise seemed to be getting closer. Lady Constance placed a hand threateningly on her scabbard. "It mystifies me, Miss Lumley, how you can even persist in calling those three untamed creatures 'children.' Just listen to them! If they dare enter my dressing room, I shall . . . I shall—why, I don't know what I shall do—"

"Excuse me, Lumawoo?"

The three Incorrigible children appeared in the doorway to Lady Constance's dressing room. They carried pencils and rulers and compasses. Alexander held several sheets of graph paper, all covered with drawings of triangles.

"Very sorry to disturb," he said with a bow.

"Salutations, noble lady! Forgive the interruption." Beowulf bowed even lower, and Cassiopeia performed a curtsy so deep she needed help to stand up again.

Sheepishly Alexander held out the paper. "Question, Lumawoo. Area of a triangle?"

"Chaos est rex regis," Beowulf added in Latin, by which he meant "confusion reigns."

Cassiopeia rolled her eyes. "No chaos. Half base times height. Easy!"

The boys still looked muddled. "But which is

height?" They turned their papers around and around, trying to figure out which point of the triangle was the top.

"That is an excellent question," Penelope said, quickly corralling the children. "If you will accompany me back to the nursery, we will discuss—"

"*Ahwoooooooooo!*"

"*Yap! Yap!*"

"*Ahwooooooooo!*"

The children looked at each other, bewildered.

"Use words, not barks?" Beowulf suggested, but to whom did he suggest it? For although these *ahwoo*s, *woof*s, and *yap*s were indisputably of a barking, howling nature—and sounded as if they were just outside the room, in fact—they were certainly not being uttered by the Incorrigibles.

From the hallway came sounds of scuffle and collision.

"Blast, blast, blast!" a man's voice cried, followed by, "*Yap!*"

Lord Fredrick lurched into the room. To Penelope he looked dreadfully uncomfortable. He scratched at himself uncontrollably, and every so often one of his legs seemed to twitch.

"I say, Constance, where's my almanac? Can't find

it for some reason. Need to check something—blasted calendar! I've mixed up the dates, I'm afraid—*woof!*"

Alexander leaned close and sniffed Lord Fredrick. He turned to his siblings and shrugged.

"Silly Fredrick, we are going to the theater; surely no one could have a mix-up about that." Lady Constance stood and twirled. "Aren't you going to compliment me on my outfit?"

"Very pretty, yes, yes." He peered at the eye patch. "But there's something on your face, dear. Might want to wash it off, *woof!*"

Lady Constance frowned. "What is that dreadful noise you keep uttering? Surely you are not making fun of me?"

"Not at all, dear. There's—*yap! woof!*—something stuck in my throat, that's all." He cleared his throat, to demonstrate, but instead of "ahem" it came out more like *"ahwoo,"* and he quickly covered his mouth.

"Well, I hope you are not going to be this noisy during the play. I simply detest it when other people talk during a performance." She swaggered past the children and fixed her one usable eye on Fredrick. "Are you ready, husband? You seem a bit . . . unkempt."

"Of course, perfectly ready"—the rubbing and scratching had made his hair stand up every which way—"but if I could just get a peek at the almanac—drat, I hope I didn't leave it at the club—"

"You can find it when we get home, silly. Now call for Timothy to bring the carriage 'round, please! And tell him we'll take the brougham; it looks terribly sharp in the daylight—"

"Already did, my dear. You might say I'm itching to leave myself, what?" Lord Fredrick commenced to rub his back against the door frame. "Where the blast is he—ow, ow, *wow bow wow*—"

A butler stepped around him and announced, "Your carriage is waiting outside, my lord."

"Got your wrap, Constance?" Lord Frederick said between scratches.

"Of course. And my sword, tee hee!" No one laughed, but Lady Constance seemed not to care; she was too busy admiring her scabbard.

"*Yap!* Pardon me!" Lord Fredrick looked embarrassed. "Blast these sneezing fits! Coming down with a bit of a cold, I'm afraid."

Penelope and the children watched Lord Fredrick in fascination. Even in the span of these few minutes, his twitching, scratching, and grunting had become more pronounced. So much so that Lady Constance, who rarely paid close attention to other people, had no choice but to notice.

"Are you all right, dear?" she asked impatiently. "You are frightfully twitchy."

He pawed frantically at his ear and peered out the window. "Bit of a rash, I think—must have been something I ate. Hours before dark yet, I see. What sort of moon are we expecting, eh? Anybody know? Would it possible to change our tickets for another night, I wonder?"

"Don't be ridiculous, Fredrick; it's the premiere! And who cares about moonlight?" Lady Constance said gaily, taking her husband's arm. "Soon we shall see all the footlights blazing!"

"Quite so, dear—*woof!* Pardon me. *Yap!*"

And with that, they left.

IN THE KITCHEN, in the laundry, in all the distant parlors of Number Twelve Muffinshire Lane, Penelope knew there were servants tending fires and trimming candlewicks, dusting shelves and sweeping carpets, filling washbasins with fresh water and emptying the old—but still the house seemed terribly quiet. As pleasant as it was to escape the grating prattle of Lady Constance and the bizarre behavior of Lord Fredrick, it also felt oddly sad to be the one left behind.

Odd, perhaps, but hardly surprising. Imagine how it would be if several people of your acquaintance purchased new outfits in anticipation of a special occasion, got dressed in a flurry of giggles and jokes, and then headed off in a group, chatting and laughing, while you remained at home in stretchy exercise pants, with nothing to do but sort socks. Penelope rarely indulged in self-pity, but now she felt as she imagined Cinderella must have, after her mean stepsisters headed out for the ball at the palace and left poor Cinderella home alone to pick lentils from the ashes.

"Yet it is only right that Lady and Lord Ashton enjoy a night out," she thought bravely. "For they are wealthy and of the noble class, and I am not. My place is here, being a good governess to the children—and answering Lady Constance's mail," she concluded with a sigh. "But answering letters is far less unpleasant than picking lentils out of ashes, so I shall do my best and try to be cheerful about it."

Penelope put the Incorrigibles to work on the letters as well—not answering them, of course, but counting them. They had carried all the mail into the dining room so as to have use of the big table; now the children were sorting the envelopes into groups of five and ten and thus got in a bit of practice with their multiplication tables. It was not nearly as much fun as a night at the theater would have been, but educationally speaking, at least the evening would not be a total waste.

Knock! Knock!

Two sharp raps at the front door echoed throughout the house.

"Not the post, again," Penelope thought as she blotted yet another letter (this one she had signed, "In spite of everything, my lips remain sealed. Yours, Lady A.") How many more letters could there be?

"Ten . . . twenty . . . thirty . . ." The children were excellent counters, which merely underscored how very many pieces of correspondence were already on hand. All this mail, and still no word from Simon, and none from Miss Mortimer either! It hardly seemed fair, and all too soon their stay in London would be over. So far their trip had not been quite the nonstop carnival of culture Penelope had hoped for, what with all the distracting danger and mystery and so on, but still, it was London, and who knew if and when she would return? The footlights of the West End might remain a distant, unfulfilled dream forevermore.

And she might never see Simon again, either. Poor Simon! She hoped he had not been convicted as a thief and transported to Australia over that silly velocipede. All his troubles had been caused by trying to be helpful to Penelope, and now she would never even get to say, "Thank you" to dear, kind, perfectly nice Simon.

"Simawoo," Alexander said.

With a twinge of embarrassment Penelope realized that she must have spoken the name aloud. "Yes, Simon," she said briskly. "Now, about those multiplication tables—"

"Simawoo," Beowulf tugged at her sleeve and pointed.

"Sim*ahwoooooo*!" Cassiopeia howled in delight.

"That's right, kids. It's me! Simawoo Harley-Dickinson, late of Scotland Yard. Good evening to you, Miss Lumley. Say, I hope you don't mind me barging in like this."

Penelope stood up. The letters in her lap fell to the floor, and her mouth fell as far open as her jaws would allow. "Mr. Harley-Dickinson! I am so very glad to see you! Are you all right? Oh, I have imagined the most dreadful things"—and she stopped right there, for she was afraid she might melt into a puddle of tears, which hardly seemed appropriate, given how happy she was.

The children felt no such confusion; all three leaped upon Mr. Harley-Dickinson as if he were a human jungle gym. He just laughed.

"I tell you, Miss Lumley, lately my life has been one dramatic plot twist after another! You're a good influence, I must say—all of you." Gently he peeled the children from his limbs. "I must apologize for missing our appointment yesterday. You see—"

"It was the velocipede!" she exclaimed.

"Indeed it was. No sooner had I completed my tour of every bookstore in London—"

"Did you find any *Hixby's*?" she blurted again.

Simon smiled. "I'm getting to that! No sooner had I finished my tour of the bookstores of London than I was stopped by a police officer. The fellow takes a long, suspicious look at my mode of transport. 'Proof of ownership!' he demands, and holds out his meaty hand, like so.

"'Now, sir,' I say, 'on what basis can you demand such proof?'

"'I'm demandin' it because this contraption matches the description of one such item reported stolen,' he says.

"'What's the description?' I say.

"Without even checking his notes, the fellow replies, 'Velocipede, slightly used. Two wheels, handlebars, black.'

"'I see,' I say. 'And when was it stolen?'

"'This very morning,' he says.

"'Well,' I say, 'here's my alibi: This morning I was out at the zoo with Judge Quinzy—a judge, mind you—and if you don't believe me, you can ask hizzoner yourself.'

"'Well,' he says, 'all right, come with me to the station house and we'll see about this Judge Quinzy of yours.' So we go to the police station. Forms are filled out in triplicate. Handcuffs applied. And I wait, and wait. After a lifetime or so, the officer comes back. 'No such judge,' he says.

"'What do you mean?' I retort. I tell you, I was miffed! No such judge? 'I rode in the bloke's carriage myself,' I say.

"And the bobby replies, 'There's no Quinzy in the *Directory of Judges*, is what I'm saying.' He showed me the book himself, and he was right. No Quinzy at all. It made my alibi sound a wee bit suspicious, and that's how I got thrown in the lockup. They only let me out because—you won't believe it—some cheeky rogue stole the velocipede! Right out of police headquarters!" Simon slapped his knee in hilarity. "No evidence, no case. They had to let me go."

"Oh, no!" Penelope was both horrified and fascinated by this strange and comical adventure. "But—handcuffs, dear me! It must have been awful!"

"Awfully interesting, more like it. What an inspiring collection of rogues I met in the clink! I've got enough material for twenty plays now." He beamed. "I tell you, Miss Lumley, ever since I met you and these charming Incorrigible children, unexpected things just keep on happening. I'll never be at a loss for words again."

"Quinzawoo, zoo, who?" Cassiopeià, asked, meaning, obviously, "If, as you say, there is no such person as Judge Quinzy, then who was the man who took us to the zoo the other day?"

"Good question, Cassawoof." Simon hoisted the girl onto his knee. "That chap we met calls himself Judge Quinzy. Whether Quinzy's his real name I can't say, but he's definitely not a judge."

Penelope was bursting to know: "And the *Hixby's*?"

His expression grew serious. "It's just as you guessed, Miss Lumley. I checked every bookshop from here to Charing Cross. There are no *Hixby's* guides, of any kind, anywhere. Nobody's ever heard of them. What you've got there is sui generis."

"Latin?" Beowulf asked excitedly.

"Clever boy! Latin it is. 'Sui generis'; it means 'one of a kind.' As for Madame Ionesco, the missing Gypsy, what with being in jail and all, I haven't been able to conduct a thorough search for her just yet. However, on the way over I did manage to come into possession of these—"

As if all the rest were not extraordinary enough, Simon now proceeded to reach into his vest pocket, from which he produced a fistful of tickets. At first Penelope was taken aback; all she could think of was that man outside Buckingham Palace, selling tickets to the pauper's food line.

"Are those—tickets?" she gasped.

"Not just tickets, Miss Lumley. Theater tickets!" He grinned. "Remember I told you I was acquainted with the stage manager at the Drury Lane? And they had a new show, opening tonight, as it happens? Apparently the King of Belgium, or Hungary, or some other midsized European nation, bought a whole box for the premiere and then canceled due to a civil war breaking out, so my friend had some extra seats to dispose of. Five, in fact."

"*Theater* tickets! You don't mean—" Penelope could scarcely believe it.

"That's right, Miss Lumley." Already the children were swaggering about like sailors; Alexander had put up a hand to cover one eye. "We're going to see *Pirates on Holiday.*"

THE FIFTEENTH CHAPTER

The audience goes wild,
and so do the actors.

"DON'T LOOK NOW, BUT EVERYTHING'S about to change,"
warned Agatha Swanburne, and the wise woman was
right as usual. The fickle Fulcrum of Fortune had
seesawed back again, this time with Penelope on the
upward-bound seat.

In terms of luck, one might say the Incorrigible
children and Simon were zooming skyward as well, for
soon they would all be enjoying the premiere performance of *Pirates on Holiday* from the luxurious comfort
of the Royal Box. Five tickets, free of charge! This was

an unexpected development indeed.

Perhaps it was the abrupt change in altitude, but Penelope was practically light-headed with joy. However, she had not completely lost her grip. She knew it was optoomuchstic to think they might get through the evening without running into the Ashtons, or to imagine that such an encounter would be anything less than extremely unpleasant. What explanation would she give for her presence at the Drury Lane Theater?

"The truth is always best," she concluded as she quickly assembled clean clothes for the children and brushed the dust off her one and only hat. And who could worry about such things now? If they were going to make the curtain, they had to leave at once. Simon assured her it would be fastest to walk, since the streets around the theater got so congested in the evenings that even the omnibus could scarcely pass. Nor was there time to feed the children a proper dinner, and the kitchen was all out of biscuits. Penelope trusted that the excitement onstage would be enough to engage their attention until snacks could be provided, after the show.

"Moon, moon, moon, moon, moon," the children counted as they marched along. Penelope assumed they were thinking of the circled dates in Lord Fredrick's almanac, but no; they were passing one of those long, rectangular, neoclassical buildings one saw so often in London, with scores of windows all in a row. Each window framed a reflection of the moon, which had risen even as they walked. It was as full as a moon could be, round as a dinner plate and glowing with an eerie blue-white light.

"Say, children," said Simon, after the "moon, moon, moon" chant began to grow tiresome. "I know another song you might like. It's about Drury Lane, and we're on our way to the Drury Lane Theater. I'll teach it to you."

He did, and now he and the children sang:

"Do you know the Muffawoo?
The Muffawoo, the Muffawoo!
Do you know the Muffawoo,
Who lives on Drury Lane? Woof!"

all the way to the theater.

Penelope did not join in. She kept glancing up at the moon, and thinking of Lord Fredrick and his odd behavior. She thought of the sui generis *Hixby's* guidebook, the fictitious Judge Quinzy, and the mysterious danger Miss Mortimer had warned her about. She thought of the Incorrigible children's "unusual background," and the long-lost Lumleys, too.

Penelope had already done quite a bit of math that day, between teaching the children how to figure the area of a triangle and performing a thorough review of the multiplication tables, but at the moment she only longed to "put two and two together," as the saying goes, and come up with some sort of answer that made sense.

Alas, the solution was not yet clear.

THERE WAS A RUCKUS OUTSIDE the lobby of the Drury Lane Theater, and it had nothing to do with muffins.

"Does anyone need a ticket?" Lady Constance Ashton cried plaintively. "For my husband was taken ill at dinner, and went home, or so he says. Personally I am not sure I believe it, for he was completely fine this morning! I think he simply does not care about attending the theater; no doubt he would rather be at his club. Ticket? Ticket, anyone? It is the premiere, and you would get to sit with me—Lady Constance Ashton, of Ashton Place—anyone?"

Perhaps it was because Lady Constance's Fulcrum of Fortune had taken a nosedive, or perhaps it was the foolish pirate outfit—for whatever reason, and despite the desirability of the ticket, Lady Constance found no takers. However, she was on the receiving end of many curious, pitying, and disdainful looks.

"That is my mistress, Lady Ashton," Penelope whispered to Simon. They were still outside the theater, hidden by the crowd, but close enough to witness this sorry spectacle. "Let us wait here a moment, until she takes her seat."

"All right," said Simon. "But she looks like she's lost at sea. Oughtn't we go over and tow her back to shore, so to speak? Maybe we could jolly her up a bit."

Penelope sighed and remembered how she had tried and failed to befriend the lady in the past. "Your suggestion is very kind, but I am afraid things are never so simple with Lady Constance."

The children started gesturing wildly. "Gypsawoo, gypsawoo!" they cried.

Penelope turned, but Simon saw her first. "Say, it's Madame Ionesco!" he exclaimed. The semitoothless old soothsayer had set up shop in the narrow alley that led to the theater's stage door. At the moment she was reading the palm of a man who was either a pirate, or an actor dressed as one. Judging from his expression, the news from the spirit world was not good. Even so, Madame Ionesco stayed in firm possession of his one hand while he dug into the pocket of his breeches with

251

the other. Finally he produced some golden (or were they gold-painted?) doubloons, which she examined thoroughly before accepting.

"Gyps*ahwooo*!" Beowulf howled, rather loudly.

Madame Ionesco looked up and saw the children. Quickly she extinguished her burning pots of incense and began packing up her tools of prognostication: her fortune-telling cards and her crystal ball, her drawstring bags filled with carved runes and the bleached bones of small, unlucky animals.

"She is leaving! We must speak to her," Penelope tried to dash toward her, but the theatergoing masses were like a tide pushing in the other direction.

Clang! Clang! An usher rang a handbell to get the crowd's attention. Then he shouted, "Last call for *Pirates on Holiday*. The show is about to begin. All ticket holders into the theater!"

Simon shoved four tickets into Penelope's hand, keeping one for himself.

"Miss Lumley, you and the children take your seats. I'll follow Madame Ionesco and make arrangements for us to meet her after the performance."

The crowd surged toward the doors; Penelope struggled to keep the children near her. "But what about *Pirates on Holiday*?"

Simon glanced over his shoulder. Madame Ionesco had folded up her stool and was now scurrying down the street. In a moment she would be gone. "What this woman knows is important, isn't it?"

"It may be. But it would be a pity for you to miss the show! You procured the tickets, after all—"

Simon shook his head. "I've seen plenty of shows. But you haven't. I'll catch the fortune-teller; you and the children enjoy the play. Don't worry, Miss Lumley. I'll be back before intermission."

Penelope watched anxiously as he fought his way against the throngs. "I hope nothing untoward happens to him this time," she thought. "After all, he is only recently out of prison."

Clang! Clang!

"All ticket holders into the theater! Last call!"

THE CROWD RUSHING INTO THE theater was like one of those strong beach currents that you can only swim along with until it decides to toss you willy-nilly onto the sand. Penelope and the Incorrigibles were caught and swept inside; they clung fast to one another just as they had in Euston Station on the day they arrived in London.

The usher looked skeptical when Penelope and the

children presented tickets that read ROYAL BOX, but he handed them programs and waved them on. Up the stairs they climbed, until another usher directed them to walk down a side aisle and through a small door. They found themselves in a private compartment of upholstered seats, almost like a train compartment but open on one side so they could watch the show, and so near the front of the auditorium as to be nearly on top of the stage.

From this crow's nest Penelope could see everyone in the audience—and everyone could see her, she realized in dismay. It would be bad enough for Lady Constance to discover her Poor Bright employee and three wild wards at the theater; it would be another degree of calamity altogether for the lady to realize they had the best seats in the house. Penelope slouched down in her seat, held up her program to shield her face, and hoped the show would begin soon.

Alas, the Incorrigibles were far too excited to hide behind programs. Alexander had brought his compass and was using it to determine the orientation of the stage. Ever interested in art, Beowulf was transfixed by the murals painted on the ceiling of the theater, which featured adorable winged cherubs playing golden harps.

Cassiopeia, whose usual bedtime was fast approaching, yawned and stretched herself out across her seat and the empty one next to it that waited for Simon. "Cassawoof tired," she complained. "Hungry. No dinner. Want snack."

"See, Cassawoof," Beowulf pointed upward. "Pigeons. Yum."

Penelope looked up, too, and saw the plump, tasty-looking cherubs, with their birdlike wings. "Oh, dear me, they are not pigeons at all—" she began to scold. But before more could be said, the footlights were lit, the curtain rose, and *Pirates on Holiday* began.

So this was the professional London theater! From the opening notes played by the orchestra, it was as if they had been whisked to another world. The actors were good, as good as Leed's Thespians on Demand, the popular troupe Lady Constance had hired to perform at the disastrous holiday ball at Ashton Place. The plot was comical and terribly convoluted, with pirates who were actually noblemen in disguise, noblemen who were being impersonated by pirates, several different intersecting love stories, a hunt for stolen treasure, and of course, eye patches, scabbards, and peg legs galore.

It was, in a word, spectacular. Penelope had not been so thoroughly entertained since reading *Jump,*

Rainbow, Jump! for the first time. That was a wonderful story, too, about how dear, sweet Rainbow got over his fear of jumping. But this was entertainment of a different stripe altogether, for on top of all the other delights unfolding on the stage, every now and then the pirates burst into song. Rainbow could whinny quite prettily on command, and always came trotting up when Edith-Anne whistled "God Save the Queen," but it was hardly the same thing.

"Lumawoo," whispered Cassiopeia. "Hungry! No dinner! Want snack now."

"Yum, yum," said Beowulf, gazing up at the murals.

Alexander used his compass to navigate. "Tasty cherub birds, north by northwest—"

"Shhh," Penelope said, unable to tear her eyes from the stage. "We shall purchase snacks at the interval. Now, let us listen to the play."

AND THEY DID, MORE OR less, and everything proceeded swimmingly, until Scene Three, when a new actor made his entrance (it might have been a her, actually, but it was impossible for Penelope to tell, for reasons about to revealed). The new actor was no more than a foot tall (not counting his—or her—tail), in bright green with scarlet and yellow markings. The garishly colored creature was perched on the first mate's shoulder. It was, in fact, a parrot.

"Surely it is only a prop parrot," Penelope told herself. But then the creature squawked and batted its wings. Nervously it twitched its head around as the lights hit it.

"Ahoy, matey!" it croaked, blinking at the audience. "Caw, caw!"

As the laughter and applause died down, Penelope thought of how the pigeons of London had tempted the children to pounce. How they had had no dinner. How Beowulf was already drooling at the sight of painted winged cherubs (who, to be fair, were very meaty and tender looking).

Suddenly alert, Cassiopeia tugged on Penelope's sleeve. "Snack?" she whispered eagerly, her eyes glued to the stage.

"It is not a snack," Penelope whispered back, as firmly as a person can whisper. "It is an actor. That parrot is a professional thespian, highly trained."

Penelope was righter than she knew. For, much as actors specialize in pretending to be that which they are not, often with the use of clever disguises, noses made of putty and inscrutable accents, this parrot, too, was pretending. It was a real parrot, make no mistake.

But it was not a pirate's parrot. It was a thespian parrot. And no parrot in the wild was likely to know how to emote in quite the way this one did—

"Ahoy, matey! *Caw caw!* Ahoy! *Ahoooooooooooooy!*"

Was Penelope imagining it? Was the parrot—this thespian parrot, impersonating a pirate's parrot, with a miniature costume eye patch covering one beady little bird eye—was this talented avian of the stage *howling*?

"Ahoooooooooooy!"

"Ahoooooooooooy!"

"Children, come with me," she ordered as she stood up and unceremoniously dragged the three Incorrigibles out of their seats.

Alexander was puzzled. "Show not over, Lumawoo."

"True, but it is nearly intermission, and if we go now we will be first in line for the biscuits on sale in the lobby." Try as she might, she could not find the exit to the Royal Box in the dark. Instead, she clambered over the side. The children were much better climbers than she was and leaped over nimbly. All four of them landed with a thud in Row K of the orchestra section, which was, of course, occupied.

"Sit down, miss, you're blocking the stage."

"Ow! Watch your step, lady! That was my foot!"

With uncharacteristic rudeness, Penelope ignored

the complaints of her fellow theatergoers, for the bizarre screeches emanating from the stage were getting louder and wolfier by the minute.

"*Ahoooooooooooy!*"

"*Ahoooooooooooy!*"

"*Ahoooooooooooy!*"

Even as Penelope dragged and cajoled them up the aisle, the eyes of the Incorrigibles remained riveted on this inexplicable bird, with its canine howls and bright green plumage, miniature peg leg, and rakish three-cornered hat.

"Alexander! Beowulf! Cassiopeia! Stay close, we must leave at once—excuse me, pardon me, we must get through—"

But it was too late.

"*Ahoooooooooooooooooooooy!*" the bird wailed.

"*Caw! Caw!*" replied Cassiopeia with enthusiasm, flapping her arms like wings. "*Ahwoooooooooo!*"

"*Ahoooooooy!*" Now the bird sounded confused.

Beowulf joined in. "*Ahwoooooooooo!*"

"*Ahoooooooooooy!*" screamed the parrot in terror.

From somewhere in the auditorium, Lady Constance Ashton stood up and yelled, "Have I gone mad, or is it those dreadful Incorrigible children? Stop! Stop it this instant! For I am developing the

"Ahooooooooooooooooooooooy!" *the bird wailed.*

most—excruciating—headache—*waaaaaaaaaaaaaah!*"

Now even Alexander could control himself no longer.

"*Ahwoooooooooo!*"

"*Ahwoooooooooo!*"

"Snack*ahwoooooooooo*!" bellowed Cassiopeia, pointing at the bird. All three children dashed for the stage, barking and growling and having what seemed to be a simply marvelous time.

If the terrified parrot harbored any plans to continue its performance, they were now abandoned. The bird shook off its eye patch and tried to take flight. Alas, one of its legs was tethered by a long, thin cord to the epaulet of the actor pirate upon whose shoulder it had so recently perched. The poor bird flapped and flapped, cawing and screeching, but since it could not escape, all its efforts merely created a flurry of green feathers flying here and there, with every move illuminated by the footlights.

Now on the stage, Alexander, Beowulf, and Cassiopeia did their best to catch the bird, which easily stayed out of reach. The pirate to whom the squawk box was attached bore the brunt of the abuse, as the parrot flapped in a panic around his head.

"Green feathers!" yelled Cassiopeia, batting the

rain of plumage from her head. "Like man on train!"

"Will no one assist us?" Penelope cried from the back of the theater, but then she remembered (as you no doubt will as well) the awful truth of the Who, Me? syndrome. With so many people watching this catastrophe unfold, the odds that any one of them would offer to help were tragically slim. In fact, most of the audience seemed to think the sudden appearance onstage of three howling children was part of the show. They sat up straighter in their seats and took out their opera glasses so as not to miss any of the action.

One of the pirates, a tall one, with dark hair and an oddly shapeless nose, raised his sword high. "Avast, ye hearties! The ship has been stormed by blackguards! Renegades! Cutthroats! Bilge rats who're yappin' and barkin' like scurvy dogs! We'll brook none o' that on my ship! Those three howlin' sprogs'll walk the plank, or I'm not yer captain!"

"Harrrrr!" the pirates roared, shaking their sabers to the rafters.

"But he is not your captain, or anyone else's," Penelope protested loudly from the aisle. "He is an actor! And not a very good one, either," she added without thinking.

A hush descended over the Drury Lane Theater.

Now Cassiopeia was standing on Beowulf's shoulders, stretching toward the bird. The parrot shrank as far from Cassiopeia's reach as it could, its claws digging deep into the scalp of the protesting actor to whom it was attached.

Alexander, who, alone among his siblings, had realized he was now making his West End debut, spoke.

"Pardon me, Captain," he said in a clear and stage-worthy voice. "Why plank?"

"Because ye scared me parrot, ye scurvy brat!" the captain roared. "Get 'em, men!"

The captain lunged. The children ran. The pirates, with swords in the air and the scent of rum on their collective breath, pursued.

"Oh, my heavens—can it be? The hunt is on!" Penelope cried, but not a soul heard her above the thunderous din of applause.

THE SIXTEENTH CHAPTER

At the mew-eezum, something
hidden is revealed.

"BRILLIANT! GROUNDBREAKING! A LAUGH a minute!" So
the members of the audience marveled to one another
as they rushed to the lobby, for they all assumed it
must be intermission. "The best first-act finale since
Attila the Hun in Iambic Pentameter. Now, shall we purchase some snacks?"

Penelope's review would have to wait. "Alexander!
Beowulf! Cassiopeia! Where have you gone? Wait! Wait
for me!" Manners forgotten, she pushed and elbowed
her way through the lobby doors and stood on Drury

Lane, frantically calling, "Children! Where are you?"

By now the pirate actors (or actor pirates, if you prefer) had also emerged from the theater, still in character, and still in pursuit of the Incorrigibles. Their cries of "Harr!" and "Scurvy brats!" rang all around her. Were they acting? Penelope could not tell. She was fearful for the children, but she was also furious to the point of being in very high dudgeon indeed. Imagine, three perfectly nice children and their governess attend the theater, which ought to be a cultural and educational experience of the highest order, and they get attacked by pirates instead! On dry land, no less!

She tugged on the tail end of the nearest pirate's bandanna and fiercely scolded, "Sir! This has gone far enough. It is obvious that you are trying to add some excitement to your premiere at the children's expense, and I find it simply unacceptable. I assure you, I will be lodging a complaint with the management."

"Harrrr!" the pirate yelled, ignoring Penelope completely. "Tharrrr they arrrrrre!"

"Wharrrrr?" Penelope replied, without thinking. The pirate talk was rather contagious.

"Tharrrrr!" He pointed his cutlass toward the street. *"Lumahwoooooooo!"*

It was the Incorrigibles!

"Say! Say, Miss Lumley! Over here!"

And Simon!

"Whoa, whoa, there! Don't just stand there, miss—unless you want to be run through by a bunch of sea knaves?"

And—Old Timothy?

It *was* Old Timothy! The Ashtons' brougham was in Drury Lane, directly in front of the theater, with Old Timothy in the driver's seat. He was having a devil of a time keeping the horses from bolting, what with all the pirates swarming about. Penelope could not have been more surprised if Agatha Swanburne herself were holding the reins.

"Easy, easy!" The old coachman's neck muscles strained to whipcords as he held the horses back. "Get in, miss, before these ruffians frighten the horses half to death! Whoa, easy—"

The carriage door opened; in a flash, Simon's hand reached out to help Penelope up. The moment she was inside, Simon called out, "All aboard! Time to set sail, and quick."

"Aye!" Old Timothy turned and cracked his whip over the heads of the pirates, to scatter the crowd.

Crack!

Then again over the horses.

266

Crack! Crack!

They reared and hit the ground at a full gallop; the carriage heaved into motion, and a bouncy, bumpy, bone-shaking ride it was. The traffic around the theater was dense, but Old Timothy drove the horses through it like a man possessed. The Incorrigibles whooped and hollered as if they had never had so much fun in their lives.

Still reeling from the shock of it all, Penelope looked around the carriage. There were Simon and all three Incorrigibles, sitting next to a heap of rags. Between whoops, the children nibbled on flat, circular cakes. Their happy faces were covered with crumbs.

"Snacks, hooray!" Cassiopeia announced, showing Penelope the half-eaten cake. Before anyone could explain, the rags spoke.

"Nice babies. Feed babies." From the midst of the pile a wide, semitoothless grin emerged, and the Gypsy revealed herself from within the camouflage of her own shawls.

The carriage lurched and swerved. Simon held on to his hat and said, "Miss Lumley, allow me to present Madame Ionesco. Prognosticator extraordinaire. Although I think you've met once before."

"How"—bump!—"do you do?" Penelope said,

astonished. "I am pleased to be properly introduced to you, madame. Though I must say, this is all rather unexpected."

"Is unexpected for me, too," the fortune-teller confided. "And I see future, so unexpected things very rare."

"Madame Ionesco was kind enough to agree to join us after the show, for a modest fee, of course," Simon explained. "We'd just concluded negotiations when we saw the children run out, and those ridiculous pirates— and then the Ashtons' driver appeared and offered to drive us all to safety."

"I knew wolf babies be at pirate show," the old woman bragged. "I saw it—here. . . ." She closed her eyes and gestured in the air, indicating the Realm of Mysterioso.

"Thankawoo for yum-yum Gypsy cakes," Beowulf said, taking another.

"You welcome, honey." Madame Ionesco seemed far better prepared for this adventure than Penelope was. Clearly, prognostication had its advantages.

"Hey!" It was Old Timothy, yelling over the clatter of galloping hooves. "Before you serve tea and crumpets, would you mind tellin' me where we're goin'?" For indeed, the pirates were still chasing them. Some were on horseback, some were on foot, and some—could it be?—were riding velocipedes.

"Harrrrr!" the pirates yelled, waving their swords.

"Ahooooooy! Caw! Caw!" The parrot had finally gotten loose from its tether and was now serving as navigator, flying after the brougham and then swooping back toward the pursuing pirates to show them which way to go.

Penelope spoke urgently to Simon. "If my understanding of theatrical custom is correct, the interval will soon be over, and the actors will have to return to the theater to perform the second act. We simply must hide until then."

"How about my garret? It's a bit downtrodden to be sure, but well off the beaten path."

Penelope frowned. "Off the beaten path is not good enough. We need someplace truly obscure."

"Little trafficked," Madame Ionesco suggested. "More cake, wolf babies?"

Little trafficked? Could that truly be what the old Gypsy had said? But no matter. Now Penelope knew exactly what to do. She laid a hand on her purse and felt the familiar outline of the *Hixby's Guide* within.

"Take us to the British Museum," she ordered the coachman. "And hurry!"

"The mew-eezum! The mew-eezum!" The children were overjoyed. First the theater, and now a trip to the British Museum; surely this had been their most educational day in London yet.

Old Timothy's cries of "hep-hep" and "hee-yah!" kept the horses at full tilt. The carriage bounced and rattled along the stony streets, at times so violently it seemed as if the wheels would shatter. At this pace Penelope knew she had only moments to ask the fortune-teller all the questions that had been wheeling through her mind.

She spoke quickly and low, so the children would not hear. "Madame Ionesco, on the day we first met, you said something to the children. 'The hunt is on.' Can you tell me what it means?"

"Shhhhh!" The Gypsy closed her eyes and made a series of strange gestures with her hands. "There is curse on the wolf babies, and on their kin," she intoned. "Terrible curse, made long before they were born."

"A curse? Madame Ionesco, that's absurd," Simon interjected.

The fortune-teller shrugged. "'The hunt is on.' See for yourself."

Penelope craned her neck out the window. That

there were throngs of rampaging actor pirates pursuing their carriage *was* thoroughly absurd, yet it seemed thoroughly dangerous, too. The costumes were silly, the accents ridiculous, but the swords were ever so sharp.

She turned back to the Gypsy. "Madame, I have been told you are a true Soothsayer from Beyond. A Seer Through the Veil. A person who can Glimpse Beyond the Mist."

"Thank you, honey." Madame Ionesco flashed her semitoothless grin. "I do my best."

"With all your powers, then—can you remove this curse?"

Madame Ionesco looked nervous. "If curse had been made by a human person, maybe. But it was not. . . ."

Penelope felt goose bumps prickle on the back of her neck. "Not human? Then what were they cursed by?"

In answer, Madame Ionesco threw back her head and howled.

"Ahwoooooooooooo!"

Beowulf and Cassiopeia joined in merrily.

"Ahwoooooooooooo!"

"Ahwoooooooooooo!"

"Mew-eezum!" Alexander announced. "Arriving now!"

271

The horses whinnied as the carriage rocked to a halt. Penelope tried to thank Old Timothy for his timely rescue, but the old coachman simply tugged at his cap and grumbled, "I'm at your service, miss—yours and the children's," which struck Penelope as a meaningful yet enigmatic sort of remark.

But any further conversation with Old Timothy would have to wait, for as soon as his passengers were out of the carriage he leaped back into his seat, grabbed the reins and the whip, and drove off at once. He was going back to the Drury Lane Theater, for there was no telling what had become of Lady Constance in all the chaos, and she was, after all, his employer.

With their rescuer gone, Penelope, Simon, Madame Ionesco, and the children were left standing at the entrance to the British Museum.

"Parthenon," said Alexander, admiring the building's design.

"Nice pediment," Beowulf observed.

"Big, big, big, big, big," said Cassiopeia, counting the row of massive fluted columns that lined the colonnade.

All three children were quite correct, for the British Museum had recently been given a new entrance that looked like something out of ancient Greece. It would have been a perfect opportunity for a lesson on the relationship between neoclassical and Greek Revival styles of architecture; alas, there was no time. They had eluded the rampaging pirates for the moment, but the theatrically inclined parrot still swooped overhead. With a mocking *"Caw! Caw! Ahoooooooy!"* it darted back the way it came.

"That parrot will lead our pursuers here within minutes. We must find Gallery Seventeen at once," Penelope said as she retrieved the *Hixby's Guide* from her purse.

Simon gazed at the imposing pillars of stone. "Say, Miss Lumley—I hate to mention it, but as it's a bit late in the evening, the museum is closed."

"Have no fear; on the subject of Gallery Seventeen, Mr. Hixby's instructions are quite thorough." She found the page and read. "'After hours, use the hidden entrance.'"

"Where hidden entrance?" Cassiopeia asked Alexander, who was already fiddling with his compass.

"I don't know, Cassawoof. Is hidden."

"Tharr!"

"Harr!"

"Ahoooooooy!" The sound of their pursuers was faint in the distance, and growing closer.

"May I?" Simon took the *Hixby's Guide* and unfolded the map. "If only I had my sextant—what do you think, Alexander?"

While Simon and the children examined the map, Penelope turned to Madame Ionesco. "I am afraid those sword-wielding thespians will be here any moment. Can you create some sort of diversion? It may buy us the time we need to escape."

The fortune-teller chuckled. "I queen of diversion. You watch."

Simon and Alexander were clearly getting nowhere; they turned the map 'round and 'round as if they were trying to find the top end of a triangle. "This map is highly detailed, but the hidden entrance does not appear to be on it," Simon said in frustration.

"I told you, is hidden," Alexander explained with a shrug.

Suddenly Beowulf let out a sharp bark to get everyone's attention. "Beowoo idea!" he exclaimed. "Follow the smell of paintings!"

Penelope and Simon exchanged a look. Beowulf clearly was being optoomuchstic, and yet—

"It's an absurd plan, but I have no better one," Simon said.

"It is worth a try, at least," Penelope agreed.

"Children, if you please: sniff!"

The Incorrigibles sniffed. They closed their eyes and sniffed again. One after another, they caught the scent.

"Oil paints!" Cassiopeia pointed.

"Turpentine!" Alexander pointed the same way.

"Ominous Landscapes—tharrr!" Beowulf cried. All three children bolted around the side of the museum.

"I make distraction! No worries! Save babies!" Madame Ionesco yelled after them. But there was no time to look back, for Penelope and Simon were already chasing after the Incorrigibles.

SNIFFING AND RUNNING AND THEN sniffing some more, they made it all the way 'round the back of the museum before finding the source of those distinctly artistic aromas: a rather ordinary-looking door tucked behind a hedge. Close inspection revealed that the door was marked with the faded numerals one and seven.

"This must be the hidden entrance to Gallery Seventeen! Well done, children." Penelope made a mental note to positively spoil the children with treats when they got home, as a reward for being so clever.

Simon pulled mightily at the door, which was stuck in the way of a door that was rarely, if ever, used.

*"This must be the hidden entrance
to Gallery Seventeen!"*

Beowulf helpfully lubricated the hinges with a bit of drool; after a "heave, ho!" from Simon and a final twist to the knob, the door creaked open.

Simon peered inside. "Bit dark in there. Better check the *Hixby's* for what to do next. I'll sneak behind the shrubbery and see how the diversion is working."

With a quiet tread born of crossing silently backstage during performances, Simon slipped behind the hedge. Penelope reached for her purse—and nearly panicked. "Who has the *Hixby's Guide*?"

"You have, Lumawoo."

"No, I am quite sure I gave it to Alexander—"

"I have compass only. Ask Beowoo?"

"Beowulf, check your pockets, please!"

"Pocket has cake crumbs, charcoal pencil, tuppence. No book."

All eyes turned to Cassiopeia. She shrugged. "Sorry. No *Hixby's*."

Penelope did a quick inhale-exhale to steady herself. "It must have been dropped in all the excitement. Never mind. We found the door to Gallery Seventeen by following the smell of paintings, but inside the museum it will smell like paintings everywhere. We shall have to devise another way to navigate—a Plan B, as it were—*eek*!"

But the rustle and crunch of breaking twigs was caused by Simon. He reemerged from the hedge, grinning from ear to ear. "The pirates found us, but Madame Ionesco has thrown them completely off course. She's holding a séance right there on the museum steps, and promised to raise the spirit of Richard Burbage, the greatest tragic actor of Shakespeare's day. Acting lessons from beyond the grave! They're all hooked. Speaking as a bard myself, I wouldn't mind hearing what Burbage has to say—"

Penelope glanced at the sky. The parrot circled high above. "I'm afraid there is no time for that. Quick, children—inside!"

The Incorrigibles obediently (and fearlessly) disappeared into the blackness. Simon hesitated. "Awfully dark in there. What does the *Hixby's* say?"

"I wish I knew," Penelope replied as she lifted her skirts and stepped in after the children.

Simon, who was not only a perfectly nice young man, but a brave and loyal one, too, shrugged and followed, and shut the door behind him.

ONE MIGHT ASSUME THAT ANY entrance (even a hidden one) to a place as splendid as the British Museum would have to be at least a little bit grand. But

Penelope, Simon, and the children found themselves in a pitch-dark tunnel that seemed more like the way to a dungeon. It was narrow, damp, and silent, except for the occasional *plunk . . . plunk . . . plunk* of water dripping. The ceiling was so low they had to crawl on all fours; even so, Penelope could not help bumping her head now and then.

She struggled to think of what advice Agatha Swanburne might have for their current predicament. As far as she knew, the wise old founder had never had to flee actors dressed as pirates by crawling through a dank, dark tunnel into the British Museum after hours.

"But if she had," Penelope thought, "no doubt she would have done it bravely and without any grumbling." So, "Be brave, children," she said aloud. "I know it is dark, but we shall reach the end soon, I am sure of it."

Of course, the Incorrigibles were not at all afraid of the dark, and were perfectly used to crawling on all fours. In fact, they were having a fine old time worming their way through the tunnel. It was their anxious governess whom Penelope was really telling to be brave. For, you see, people of particular pluck are no different than the rest of us. At times they feel afraid, or lonely, or hopeless, just as the less plucky do; they simply happen to excel at keeping their spirits up in a pickle. As Agatha Swanburne said, "No panicking, no complaining, no quitting"—six words to the wise that are well worth learning, and following.

Simon must have felt a similar need to buck himself up. "We're almost there, Miss Lumley," he called encouragingly from somewhere behind. Penelope appreciated the sentiment, of course, but the remark made her rather glad it was too dark to see, for the rear view of her crawling along on hands and knees would have been ungraceful, to say the least.

"Thank you, Mr. Harley-Dickinson. Oh! Mr. Harley-Dickinson!"

"What?"

"Given the perilous circumstances—*ow!*—I think you might call me Penelope, if you like."

"Right-oh! Well! Call me Simon, then."

She was just as glad he could not see her blush, and smile.

IF YOU HAVE EVER HAD the misfortune to be stuck crawling through a pitch-dark tunnel without the option of turning back, with no idea if and when this nerve-racking experience might come to an end, you already know that even five minutes of such an exercise is bound to feel like a very long time indeed.

Penelope, Simon, and the Incorrigibles crawled heroically along for nearly twice that long, and one can only imagine what an eternity it seemed to them. But there is an old saying (not one of Agatha Swanburne's, as it turns out, although she would have found it perfectly sensible) that insists that most tunnels do eventually have a light at the end of them, even if that end is far, far away.

This particular tunnel did not contradict the notion, for eventually the five explorers emerged into what seemed to be a dense, velvety soft thicket. They were still in the dark, but at least they could stand up. And when they pushed through the thicket (which soon revealed itself to be a tangle of heavy velvet drapes), there was not only light, but art.

Beowulf sniffed deeply. "Oil paints," he said with satisfaction. On every wall hung Historical Portraits so shameless in their Overuse of Symbolism that any first-year art student could have deduced where they were. Penelope had taken three semesters of art appreciation at the Swanburne Academy, so she had no doubt whatsoever.

"Gallery Seventeen: Overuse of Symbolism in Minor Historical Portraits," she announced, stomping the muck from her damp shoes. "We have arrived!"

Truly, it looked as if no one had ever set foot in this gallery before. A layer of dust filmed the floor, and cobwebs drifted in every corner. There seemed to be no way in or out of the gallery other than that horrible tunnel. But someone, at some point, had hung up all these frankly uninspired paintings. Why bother, if no one was ever going to see them?

They moved from portrait to portrait; at each one, Simon read aloud from the accompanying plaque. "The Chief General of Bavaria," he said. "The Regent of Lichtenstein. The Wazir of Constantinople." Even through a coat of grime the slapdash quality of the paintings was evident, with their stiff, awkwardly posed figures and dizzying parade of symbols. One could scarcely see past all the crowns, roses, shamrocks, halos, piles of gold, angel wings, laurel leaves, roaring lions—the list went on and on.

"The Goddess Diana," Simon read, as they gathered in front of the last, and strangest, painting.

"Athens and Sparta?" guessed Alexander.

"In a way. The Greeks called her Artemis, but the Romans called her Diana. See the bow and arrow, the forest in the background, the crescent moon in the sky, the litter of wolf cubs at her feet? It's Diana, all right,"

"The Wazir of Constantinople."

Simon explained. "Goddess of the hunt, of the forest, and the moon. Protector of children, too."

"Look," exclaimed Beowulf. "Ominous!"

"I know it's gloomy, but don't be frightened," said Simon comfortingly. "It's only a painting, after all."

"No, Ominous Landscape. In attic! Same Ominous." Beowulf sounded completely sure of himself, for he did have a keen eye for art.

Penelope looked at the canvas: the colors, the brushstrokes, the composition. A shiver of recognition ran down her spine. Except for the presence of Diana in the place of the bloody-fanged wolf, this painting was remarkably similar to the one at Ashton Place.

"Beowulf is right," she said, "This is by the same artist who painted a rather disturbing mural in the attic of Ashton Place."

"*Aaaaaaaaaa,*" Cassiopeia moaned.

Penelope laid a soothing hand on her head. "I know it is an important discovery, but this is no time for howling, dear."

"Aaaaaaaaa. Cursive. Look," the girl said, pointing at the lower right corner of the canvas, where artists often sign their work. Barely visible beneath the dust was the letter A, in an ornate script.

"Say, that's a funny coincidence! The ticket envelope

my acquaintance at the Drury Lane gave me, the one that had our tickets to the premiere—it had that same sort of fancy A marked on it. . . ."

Penelope only half heard Simon's musings, for her gaze was drawn back to the face of Diana. "I have seen that woman before—but where?" she murmured.

Beowulf firmly shook his head. "Ominous Landscape. Mythic lady. Wrong gallery," he concluded.

He would have been right, too, if the goddess Diana had simply been plopped in the middle of an Ominous Landscape. Then the painting would have belonged in Gallery Eleven, Use of Mythic Figures in Ominous Landscapes.

Yet this painting was, in fact, a portrait (which is to say, a picture of a real person, not a made-up one). The realization struck Penelope with the strength of an epiphany. True, this "Diana" looked quite a bit younger, but Penelope had gazed so many times at the image that hung in Miss Mortimer's study at school, she knew there could be no mistake.

It was Agatha Swanburne. There she was: the pretty, no-nonsense features, the impish yet wise expression in those wide, sea green eyes, the smooth, distinctively auburn-colored hair—

Penelope gasped.

"What is it, Lumawoo?" Cassiopeia was at her side in an instant.

"See ghost?" asked Beowulf.

"Burbage, maybe?" added Alexander hopefully. Truth be told, he had rather enjoyed his brief moment of speaking on the professional stage.

"No—not a ghost," Penelope said, after a moment. But the skin on the back of her neck prickled, and her arms were covered with goose bumps.

For receiving a message, of a sort, from a person who is long dead—why, if that did not count as seeing a ghost, then what did?

THE SEVENTEENTH AND FINAL CHAPTER

A dreadful faux pas leads
to a hasty retreat.

To KNOW WHERE YOU ARE going is always a great comfort to travelers, which is one reason that skilled navigators were as highly prized in Miss Penelope Lumley's day as those clever, robot-voiced, direction-giving gadgets are today. It also explains the enduring popularity of guidebooks, and the fact that crawling back through that dark, damp tunnel was not nearly as frightening as the first trip had been. This time Penelope, Simon, and the Incorrigibles knew precisely where they would end up.

Soon they were outside the museum once more. Just

287

as they had hoped, the sword-wielding thespians had scattered; presumably they had returned to the Drury Lane Theater to perform the second act of *Pirates on Holiday.* Madame Ionesco had disappeared as well. Penelope wondered if the pirates' second-act performances would be at all improved by their lesson with Richard Burbage, but alas, she would not be there to see it.

"Ah, well," she thought to herself, with a twinge of disappointment. "Half of a West End premiere is better than none, I suppose. The important thing is that the Incorrigibles are safe from those silly pirates. And we did manage a trip to the British Museum, finally! The children will have much to write about in their journals tonight."

The children, indeed. Their russet hair looked almost gray in the color-stealing light of the moon, but each time they passed beneath a street lamp the auburn sheen glowed like an ember. It was same color as her own natural, unpoulticed hair, and of Agatha Swanburne's, too. What could it mean? The whole moonlit walk back to Muffinshire Lane, Penelope looked at the Incorrigible children with fresh eyes.

Alexander, Beowulf, and Cassiopeia. Lost, or perhaps stolen, from their parents. Left in the woods at Ashton Place—but by whom?

Improbably, unexpectedly found by Lord Fredrick Ashton, and taken in as his wards.

Then, of all the governesses in the wide, unfathomable world, Miss Penelope Lumley, of the Swanburne Academy for Poor Bright Females, had been chosen to raise them, educate them, and as she now understood better than ever, protect them from harm.

Somehow, it was all connected. *They* were all connected; she and the children, and perhaps even Agatha Swanburne, too. But how? What did Miss Mortimer know that Penelope did not? And how did this inhuman curse that Madame Ionesco spoke of figure into things?

"Moon, moon, moon," the children chanted expectantly as they marched home. And then, "Where moons?" they wondered. For now that the hour was late, the full moon had risen too high in the sky to be reflected in the windows of the buildings. The glass rectangles were dark as inky pools.

"And now there is this business of the paintings to puzzle over as well," Penelope mused. She recalled the night she and the children had discovered that strange mural in the attic of Ashton Place. She thought of the mysterious howling sound that they had faintly heard from some hidden place behind the wall.

"What is the connection?" She scrunched her

eyebrows together, to better summon her powers of deduction. "What, what, what?"

"Moon, moon, moon," the sleepy children mumbled. It had been a very long day; Cassiopeia had run out of pep completely and was now riding on Simon's shoulders.

"Moon?" Penelope realized, with growing excitement. "Moon, moon, moon!" Yes! For it had been a full moon the night of the Christmas ball, and it was a full moon now, on the night of the *Pirates on Holiday* premiere.

Both nights had ended in mayhem, with the children being pursued—or hunted, if you will.

Lord Fredrick had been absent from both occasions: the holiday ball and the premiere.

And, earlier that very night, Penelope had gotten a howlingly good clue as to why.

"Either there were wolves living in the attic," she thought, recalling Lord Fredrick's bizarre behavior, "or Lord Fredrick was hiding inside, having a peculiar fit of itching, barking, and howling that is in some way related to the full moon!"

"Voilà!" she exclaimed, feeling thoroughly pleased with herself.

Simon and the children looked at her questioningly.

"No French lesson, Lumawoo. Too tired," Cassiopeia begged.

Penelope smiled. "French can wait until tomorrow. I merely had an epiphany of sorts, about something I have been wondering about for some months. Now, shall we sing that muffin man song as we walk?" Unlike the children, Penelope was feeling quite energetic all at once. "It is a lively little tune, and will keep our spirits up. Look, everyone, we are almost home!"

"Voilà," as you may already know, is a French word that means "there you are." Like "Eureka" or "By Jove, I've got it," "voilà" is sometimes exclaimed by people who have figured out the answer to some sort of problem or riddle that has been vexing them to no end.

But why would Penelope use a French word like "voilà" when she was nowhere near France? It is a reasonable question, and the answer is this: There are French words and phrases that only French-speaking people use, and there are French words and phrases that everyone uses. This is because some ideas are so perfectly described *en français* that no other language dares try to top it.

As an example, consider the phrase "joie de vivre." It means "the joy of living," and refers to the kind of cheerful, nonstop zest for life that stops just short of optoomuchism and makes a person a sheer pleasure to be around. "Gauche" means terribly awkward. A "provocateur" is a person who tries to stir up trouble. And then there is "faux pas," which is an embarrassing blunder or lapse of good manners.

Translated into English, "faux pas" means "false step," but faux pas are done all the time. Everyone makes mistakes now and then. Simple errors can be fixed with an eraser; more complicated blunders require an apology and a sincere effort to make things right. Either way, most mistakes are soon both forgiven and forgotten; they are a fact of life, and one ought not to lose sleep over them.

Sometimes, however, for no reason that science can yet explain, a perfectly ordinary faux pas is not forgotten at all. It becomes the subject of gossip and soon attracts the attention of the media, after which it escalates into a crisis of vast and humiliating proportions.

Alas, the newspaper that was delivered to Number Twelve Muffinshire Lane the morning after the premiere of *Pirates on Holiday* contained reports of just such a faux pas, one that was already well on its way to causing embarrassment on a global scale.

It was not part of the paper's scathing review of the

show itself (which, despite the enthusiasm of the audience, was deemed "A colossal failure, sure to fold in a week, what were they thinking?" by the *Times*'s chief theater critic, who had never been wrong about such things—although, to be fair, the critic also wrote that "some unexpectedly fine acting in the second half was not enough to salvage this barnacle-encrusted wreck of a show").

No, the *scandale du jour* was reported on the *Times* society page, which, after a few lines speculating about why the King of Belgium was a no-show, devoted the rest of the column to mocking the tasteless garb worn to the premiere by one Lady Constance Ashton.

"What I fail to understand is how the Incorrigible children could behave so abominably, and yet all they care to criticize is *my* outfit!" Lady Constance had read and reread the society page so many times and dropped so many salty tears upon it, she now had black ink smudges all over her hands and face. "Fredrick, listen to this: 'Clearly unused to London's citified ways, the childlike (or is she just simple?) Lady Ashton attended the theater in the most absurd fancy dress imaginable. A word to the wise: Only the actors wear costumes, dear!'

"And this: 'Lady Ashton's pirate getup was so gauche as to be illegal; quick, somebody, throw her in the brig!'

"You missed one, dear." Lord Fredrick shook open the business section of the London *Times*, drew it close enough to see, and read, "'The London stock market showed modest gains yesterday—and speaking of stock, Lady Constance Ashton was the laughingstock of the West End last night—'"

"Enough!" she shrieked, and buried her head in her hands, weeping.

It got worse. The eleven o'clock post brought floods of mail, as did the next post and the one after that. Letter after letter arrived, all addressed to Lady Ashton, and all withdrawing the social invitations that had so recently been extended. Plans had changed, unexpected houseguests had arrived, hosts had suddenly contracted malaria, dangerous tornadoes were expected—the excuses piled on.

None of the date cancelers was so bold as to pin it on the eye patch, but the message was clear: Because of a single, rhinestone-studded faux pas, overnight Lady Constance had become a "social pariah," which is to say, the sort of person absolutely no one who cared deeply about being popular would have anything to do with.

"Now, now, dear. It will soon blow over, what?" Lord Fredrick looked a bit worse for wear himself, with scratches on his hands and face and a lingering tendency to clear his throat in a particularly barky way, but at least the itching and howling seemed to have subsided. "The papers are just having a bit of fun, that's all. Can't take it personally, what?"

PENELOPE, TOO, WAS IN A bit of muddle. She and the children had made it home without incident. Simon— she called him Simon now, imagine that!—had parted with fond good-nights and mutual words of admiration for each other's pluck in a tough spot. She had slept like a rock and dreamed only of alpine meadows filled with appealing little songbirds.

But now it was morning, and she had to decide what to say to Lady Constance about the previous evening's mishaps. Rather than wait around to be fired, or for Lady Constance to threaten to ship the children off to an orphanage or dump them back in the forest (as she had quite rudely proposed after the wreckage of the holiday ball), Penelope wanted to take the bull by the horns, matadorlike, as it were, and offer her own side of the story. For, really, who had ever heard of a parrot trained to howl? Some provocateur was behind it all, and the children could hardly be blamed—at least, not entirely.

She sent word through Mrs. Clarke, requesting an audience, but no reply was forthcoming. It seemed Lord Fredrick was spending the day at home for a change; he and Lady Constance had not left their private rooms since the arrival of the morning paper.

"Perhaps he is still in the throes of his moon-induced 'condition.' If so, at least it is keeping him near his wife," Penelope thought. "No doubt she will be in a better mood because of this much-overdue attention, and our conversation will not be difficult." Was she being optoomuchstic? The possibility did not cross her mind.

Finally, well after teatime, Penelope received word that Lord and Lady Ashton would receive her. She smoothed her drab, blackberry-colored hair and proceeded to the dining room. There was a large pile of unopened mail on the table, near Lady Constance. With a maniacal look in her eye, Lady Constance slit open each letter, quickly skimmed its contents, and then proceeded to tear it into bits, which she carelessly let fall to the floor. By this time there was a snowdrift of torn-up paper heaped around her chair.

Lord Fredrick sat at the far end of the table with a hot-water bottle on his head, an ice pack pressed against his eyes, a glass of schnapps in front of him, and a small pill bottle of headache lozenges next to the schnapps.

Too nervous to wait to be asked to sit, Penelope began to explain and apologize the moment she entered the room. Lady Constance simply opened and ripped, opened and ripped, like a human shredding machine. When Penelope finished speaking, Lady Constance stood. She handed Penelope what was left of the society page of the *Times*, which of course Penelope had not seen, as it had been in Lady Constance's agonized clutches since the moment it arrived.

Lady Constance waited as Penelope digested the awful contents of the page. Then she spoke.

"Miss Lumley. I will be blunt. Last night was the worst night of my life. My humiliation is complete; my friends have cut me off, and my reputation is in a shambles. I am convinced it was no accident. Someone is to blame." Her eyes narrowed. "And I know exactly who is responsible."

"You do?" Penelope was amazed to hear it. Were all the many mysteries that had accumulated since their arrival in London about to be solved?

"Yes, I do," affirmed Lady Constance. "The source of all my troubles, past, present, and future, is those three . . . Incorrigible . . . children!"

"The children? But they had nothing to do with . . ."

Penelope might have said, "your ill-chosen outfit, the rudeness of the gossip columnist, and the faithlessness of your so-called friends," but she did not, for Lady Constance was clearly in no mood to hear the truth.

"Of *course* it was the children!" the lady declared. "Nothing good happens when they are near. They are unbearable! Intolerable! Incorrigible!" She turned to her husband, who had his feet propped on the table and looked only half conscious. "If only you had been there, Fredrick! You would have seen how wild and uncontrollable they were—why, they actually stormed the stage and attacked the pirates! They disrupted the performance completely."

Lord Fredrick yawned, then grunted from beneath his ice pack. "If I were a lad and stumbled across a gang of pirates it'd be bad enough, but if the ruffians burst into song—why, I'd be scared out of my wits! I'd probably start shooting just to settle my nerves, what?"

"Hmph!" Lady Constance retorted. Lord Fredrick lifted the corner of the ice pack and looked at Penelope with one eye; she could not help thinking it was rather as if he were wearing an eye patch himself.

"About those Incorrigibles—no loss of property? No damages to the wolf children? I've still got three of them, what?"

"Yes, Lord Ashton," Penelope replied. How could he speak in such a careless way about the children? It never ceased to astonish her.

"That's all right, then." He yawned again, then groaned, then popped a lozenge in his mouth and washed it down with a sip of schnapps. "But Constance, dear. Given all this unpleasantness, what say we go home to Ashton Place? I'm done with London myself. Much rather be out in the woods, shooting, what?"

Lady Constance snatched the society page back from Penelope, tore it to bits, and threw the pieces to the floor on top of all the rest of the mess. "A brilliant suggestion! We will leave at once." She ran to the bell and pulled on it repeatedly as she spoke. "Paupers! Pirates! What a dreadful place London is. Wild horses could not induce me to return to this inhospitable city—Mrs. Clarke!"

The ringing and yelling continued until Mrs. Clarke arrived, not flustered and panting as she usually would be, but in her own time and with a serene expression on her face.

"Good afternoon, my lady. Dear me, what a mess of paper! Do you need help cleaning it up?"

"I have no intention of cleaning it up," Lady Constance replied, momentarily thrown. "I merely summoned you to announce: We are leaving!"

"Are you, now?" Mrs. Clarke nodded and smiled. "Where are you going, then?"

"No, no, no! We are *all* leaving! We are returning to Ashton Place at once. Have the servants pack up the house. Why we ever came to London to begin with I cannot say; it has been a nightmare from start to finish, and I for one have had quite enough."

"All of us? At once?" Penelope repeated. Her mind raced; surely she would get the chance to say good-bye to Simon? And Miss Mortimer had not yet replied to her letter—why, she had not even met the children yet—

"Yes, all of us, much as I would like to leave you and those Incorrigible creatures behind." She glanced at the half-asleep Lord Fredrick, and lowered her voice. "And remember, my dear friend Baroness Hoover knows of some very fine orphanages for the poor. Take care, Miss Lumley—take care you do not lose your pupils to one of them!"

LADY CONSTANCE MAY HAVE WISHED to leave at once, but packing up a household is not done by wishing. And Mrs. Clarke did not panic and hurry the servants along the way she might once have done. Sure enough, staying calm and taking one's time made the work go that much faster, for without all the scolding and rushing there were fewer mistakes made and everyone kept in good spirits.

Even so, it was another few days before the house was ready to be closed up. Penelope and the Incorrigibles made good use of the time. They explored London's sights at their leisure, without worrying too much about plans or maps, or even if the walks they took were particularly educational. The children, it must be said, liked the parks best, and Penelope did manage to purchase a pretty straw hat with a long pink ribbon that looked quite striking against her dark hair.

Finally it was time to bid the grand city farewell. Lady Constance and Lord Fredrick went ahead in their brougham, driven by Old Timothy, of course. The servants would stay until the very last spoon was polished and put away. Then they would take the train home, packed together like sardines in the third-class car.

Penelope insisted on packing up her own things and the children's, too, their books and triremes and the many pages of their journals. She also had a good-bye to say, and a long-overdue errand to run; as it happened, both tasks were accomplished on her very last afternoon in London.

"Say, I wonder if the queen actually reads them all?" Simon remarked as Penelope dropped her letter in the suggestion box at Buckingham Palace.

"She must," Penelope said firmly. "For she is a good queen, and that means she must be curious to know what goes on outside the palace, as well as within." She gazed across the magnificent plaza that led to the palace gate. The paupers' food line was still there, queuing up patiently around the side of the palace: the young, the old, the in-between, all just as hungry and downtrodden as ever.

"'The royal house is warm and fine, the cold and hungry wait in line,'" Beowulf recited solemnly.

Simon turned to him, impressed. "That's a neat little poem. Did you just think of it?"

Beowulf shook his head. "Guidebook," he explained.

"It was from the *Hixby's Guide* entry on Buckingham Palace," Penelope said. "Dear old *Hixby's*. Isn't it odd? The book was scarcely any use at all, but I feel a bit at sixes and sevens without it."

"I'd offer to get you a replacement, but we both know it's not an option." Simon frowned. "Awfully sorry it got lost, Miss Lumley—I mean, Penelope. It wasn't the most practical volume, but there was something rather charming about it. I liked it."

"I liked it, too. Although the advice about following the smell of elephants did nearly get me run over by a carriage." At that Simon looked confused, for of course he did not know the part about the elephants. "In any case," she quickly went on, "we are on our way home and won't be needing a guidebook anymore."

Beowulf had brought some paper and a box of charcoal pencils with him so he could make a few final sketches of Buckingham Palace, or so Penelope thought. He took this opportunity to show her his work; as it turned out, he had spent the time drawing delightful alpine scenes.

"How wonderful." Penelope admired the drawings. "Did you draw these because the *Hixby's* book is lost, and you were trying to re-create some of the pictures?"

He nodded shyly. Alexander peered over his brother's shoulder at the picture and pointed to the flowers in the meadow. "Edelweiss," he said.

"Say, that's clever!" Simon exclaimed. "Miss Lumley's got you learning a bit of German, does she?"

Now it was Penelope's turn to look confused.

"Why, no. It would be a fine language to study, but I do not know any German at all. Do you?"

Simon gave a humble shrug. "Not really. Just enough to read bits of melancholy poetry here and there. Always had a taste for it, for some reason."

"Then I must show you my favorite poetry book," she said excitedly. "I have had it since I was a girl. It is an English translation, of course, but you might be familiar with the originals. My favorite is called 'Wanderlust'—"

"Say, I think I know that one," he said. "Something about a meadow, right?"

A distant church bell tolled the hour.

Clang! Clang! Clang! Clang!

"Four o'clock, so soon." Simon observed. "But 'Time and tide wait for no man.' That's an old sailor's saying."

"What does it mean, Simawoo?" Cassiopeia asked.

"I am afraid it means we ought to go," Penelope said reluctantly. Before Simon could offer to escort them, she went on, "If you do not mind, I should like to say our good-byes here." She was in no hurry to part, of course, but she did not want to become overly emotional in front of the children, either. Somehow, the sight of those stoic palace guards made her buck up a bit, with their imperturbable faces and brave fur hats. With the guards close by she felt she could get through it without melting into sniffles, or worse.

"All right, then. It was lovely meeting you all." Simon sounded flustered, and kept staring at his shoes. "Perhaps you'll come to London again sometime? Or perhaps not, considering all the excitement. But with any luck, we shall meet again."

"I do hope so," Penelope said, with feeling. "Ashton Place is not so very far, by train."

"Maybe I'll pop in, next time I'm heading out to see my great-uncle Pudge at the Ancient Mariner's Home. It's in the same direction, more or less."

"North by northwest?" Alexander guessed.

"Thataway!" Cassiopeia pointed.

"More or less." Simon grinned sheepishly. "All right, then. Safe travels to you. Good luck and fair winds. Thanks for the inspiration. Cheers." Simon's feet seemed stuck to the ground by some stretchy, gummy substance; he kept picking them up as if to go, and then putting them back where they had just been.

"*Viel Glück!*" Alexander added. "*Danke! Auf Wiedersehen!*"

"Aren't you a clever *Junge*?" Simon ruffled his hair. "Smart boy!"

Alexander beamed and waved. With a tug on his hat, Simon finally managed to make his exit.

After he was gone from sight, Penelope thought that she might write some melancholy poetry herself.

Cassiopeia noticed her governess's mood right away. "Lumawoo sad?" she asked, concerned. "Simon good-bye?"

"No, not sad, Cassawoof." Forgetting her professional distance for once, Penelope scooped the girl up in her arms. "I am pleased to be going home, in fact, and as for Mr. Harley-Dickinson—what could be more pleasant than making a new friend?"

LATER, AFTER ALL THEIR THINGS were packed for the morning train and the Incorrigibles were put to bed, Penelope took out her favorite poetry book and read:

"I wander through the meadows green,
Made happy by the verdant scene."

What a coincidence that Simon should know "Wanderlust"! It was hardly as popular as "To a Mouse," by Mr. Robert Burns, or even "The Wreck of the Hesperus," by Mr. Henry Wadsworth Longfellow—another particular favorite of the children's. In fact, "Wanderlust" would be considered obscure and little trafficked, as poems go. But unexpected things had become such a frequent occurrence lately, nothing really surprised Penelope anymore.

Was it optoomuchstic to think that her friendship with Mr. Harley-Dickinson—with Simon, that is—would be able to continue? Penelope certainly had her own opinion on the subject, but as Agatha Swanburne once said, "Time will tell, but only in hindsight, for time is not talking just yet."

All in all, it had been a very educational trip.

Epilogue

At Ashton Place the mail came only once a day. It was a simple, reliable system, and now that they were home, Penelope realized she much preferred it to the constant flurry of postal deliveries they had endured in London. For what mattered most about any letter was how one felt about the sender and the news he or she had to share, not how many hundreds of invitations one could brag about receiving.

Ten days after their return to Ashton Place, two letters came, both addressed to Penelope. The first was on the most elegant stationery Penelope had ever seen.

To my loyal subject, Miss Penelope Lumley,

Thank you for sharing your concerns in the suggestion box. We were not at all amused to hear that scoundrels were attempting to make a profit off the pauper's food line tickets. I have instructed the palace guard to put a quick end to any further attempts to exploit this charitable service.

I was intrigued by your idea that something more substantial be done to improve the lot of the poor so that they were, in fact, no longer poor. I am not sure how this could be accomplished. However, I shall consider it.

Miss Lumley, I can tell from your clear thinking, good grammar, and tidy penmanship that you are a superior governess; this reflects well upon your own education. I will be sure to seek out graduates of your alma mater should the palace ever require additional staff to care for the princes and princesses. They can be quite a handful.

Your Faithful Sovereign,
Queen Victoria

"Well! It is not every day one gets a letter from the queen," Penelope thought with satisfaction. "And it is good news for the Swanburne Academy, too. I shall have to let Miss Mortimer know."

Speaking of Miss Mortimer, the second letter was, in fact, from her.

My dear Penny,

How delightful it was to see you in London! I deeply regret we did not have the opportunity to meet again while you were in town. Soon after our scrumptious meal at the Fern Court I was called away on family business. I am sorry for the delay in responding to your letter, which had been forwarded from my London hotel and which I only received this morning, upon my return to dear old Swanburne. I am especially sorry that I did not get to see the children. I will, in the not too distant future. That is a promise.

By now you have likely returned to Ashton Place. At the risk of sounding like a nagging headmistress (though of course, that is exactly what I am!), I want to remind you again to use the hair poultice on schedule. The importance of maintaining a healthy scalp is not to be sneezed at, and lice are no picnic either.

About the other matters we spoke of, some of which you raise rather forcefully in your letter—Penelope, I must apologize. I see now that I was being "optoomuchstic" in thinking I could squelch your natural curiosity and powers of deduction. You are not a child anymore, and you must follow your brave heart where it leads you. But be careful. Keep your curiosity within reason, and do not let your questions go overboard. Any further visits to the attic of Ashton Place, in particular, would be taking things much too far!

At lunch, you asked me a question regarding the possibility of inquiries being made for you at Swanburne. Upon reflection, I believe I owe you a fuller answer. I will tell you this: the "persons of interest" have not forgotten you. In fact, they recently sent you a collection of picture postcards, though of necessity it had to be disguised as something else. Think about it, Penelope; you will surely understand what I mean.

I do hope the guidebook proved to be of use.

Yours,
Miss Mortimer

Picture postcards? She meant the *Hixby's Guide*, of course!

The *Hixby's Guide* was from her parents! The long-lost Lumleys, now a little less lost!

And it was gone!

Penelope did not care.

"It was from my parents," she thought, luminous

with joy. "I held it in my hands! I looked at the drawings, page by page. I remember each one: the lakes, the mountains, the ibex, that funny-looking mountain squirrel." How she wished she might see those pictures, and perhaps hug the book to her, one last time!

"But I wonder why it had to be disguised? And where the Lumleys—I mean, my parents—are now?" How strange it was that Penelope could scarcely remember her mother and father, or the home they must have once shared. "North, south, east, west—where could they be?"

NAVIGATION, YOU SEE, IS NOT just a problem for sailors. Everyone must go adventuring sooner or later, yet finding one's way home is not easy. Just like the North Star and all its whirling, starry brethren, a person's idea of where "home" is remains in perpetual motion, one's whole life long.

Home was more than a house, even if the house was very grand. The Ashtons had lived in Ashton Place for generations, but Lord Fredrick seemed loathe to spend time there. Whereas Penelope knew quite well that home was not a fixed point on a map. Home used to be the Swanburne Academy and Miss Mortimer; now it was wherever the Incorrigibles were, and wherever her favorite books were. If the place was equipped with a cozy chair to read in, so much the better.

"London was certainly a marvelous adventure, but it is good to be back at Ashton Place," she thought. And even with so many mysteries left to solve, just knowing that her parents were alive, somewhere, thinking of her, made Penelope feel more settled than even the most soothing cup of tea ever could. It made her feel at home inside herself, which is a very good thing to feel.

She thought of these things the whole rest of the day, and when the Incorrigibles wanted to hear "To a Mouse" one more time (for the Incorrigible children of Ashton Place liked to hear their favorites read aloud over and over again, just as children do to this very day), Penelope's interpretation was a wee bit more philosophical than it usually was.

"So you see, the poor mousie lost her home when the poet plowed over it, but that does not mean she has no hope of ever having a home again. It simply means she will build a new one. And who knows—it might even prove nicer than the one that was lost," she added. "What do you children think would make a good home?"

"Bouncy beds!" said Alexander, who often had to be reminded not to jump on his.

"Friends," suggested Beowulf, holding up *A Friend*

for Rainbow, from the Giddy-Yap, Rainbow! books that Penelope kept on the nursery shelf.

"Friends, of course," Penelope agreed, thinking of Simon, and Miss Mortimer. Yes, friends were absolutely essential to feeling at home.

"Pets, pets, pets," Cassiopeia said as she fed treats to an ecstatically chirruping Nutsawoo. The overjoyed squirrel had been spoiled rotten since the children's return from London; he showed no interest in the journals and postcards, except to chew on the corners, but kept coming back to the nursery window to beg nibbles of the flat, round Gypsy cakes Mrs. Clarke had asked the kitchen to prepare, since the children liked them so much.

"Bouncy beds, friends, pets, good things to eat." Penelope closed the collection of Mr. Burns's poetry that she had been reading from. "That sounds like a fine home indeed."

"And Lumawoo!" all three children piped, falling upon her.

"Hugs, not licks," Penelope reminded them, but she could not help laughing. The children obeyed, for the most part. And Penelope, who tended to be cheerful in any case, felt happier than—well, happier than she could recall feeling in a very long while.

The UNSEEN GUEST

"Lumawoo, look. What bird?"

"That, I believe, is a nuthatch—Beowulf, do be careful!" Beowulf Incorrigible was leaning so far out the nursery window that his governess, Miss Penelope Lumley, was afraid he might tumble out.

"Nuthatch? Not warbler?—*awk!*" Beowulf's reply rose into a birdlike squawk, as Penelope seized her student firmly by the ankles and returned him to a more secure position behind the windowsill. The bird in question—and on second glance, it did seem to Penelope as if it might be more along the lines of a warbler—cocked its head to one side, as if to say, "I know what I am, but what are you?" Then it pertly flitted off.

"Whether it is a nuthatch or a warbler is perhaps a matter for debate," Penelope said briskly, as she shut the wide-open nursery windows and fastened the latch for good measure, "but you, Beowulf Incorrigible, are not any kind of bird. Under no circumstances are you to fly out the window."

"Sorry, Lumawoo." The boy cast a longing glance in the direction of the bird's departure, but he did not argue. Instead, he retreated to the farthest corner of the nursery, where he began building tall, wobbly towers out of square wooden blocks that he then proceeded to tip over with barely a hint of satisfaction.

Penelope returned to her seat and tried to resume reading. But the nursery felt stuffy all at once, without the wonderful summer breeze that had been making the curtains billow and dance all morning. Beowulf's elder brother, Alexander, had spent the last hour pretending that the wind-filled curtains were sails on a ship. Their sister, Cassiopeia, had volunteered to act as a lookout against pirates, while Alexander stood manfully upon the bridge of his imaginary vessel, happily navigating away with the shiny brass sextant that was now his favorite possession.

With the closing of the windows, that game, too, had come to an end.

"No wind," Alexander announced, wetting his finger and holding it in the air as a test. "We are becalmed. Drop anchor, mate."

"Aye aye, Captain. Seasick, anyway." Cassiopeia obeyed but sounded glum. She was the youngest of the three Incorrigible children, and, it could be argued, the wildest. Truth be told, she had been rather hoping for a run-in with pirates, for she held a bit of a grudge against them ever since the Incorrigibles' recent trip to London, and was hoping to get "last licks," as they say nowadays.

(The theatergoers among you may be able to hum a few bars from *Pirates on Holiday*, the seaworthy operetta whose disastrous premiere the Incorrigibles and their governess had had the great misfortune of attending during their stay in London. If so, you will have some idea of why Cassiopeia felt the way she did. If not, it is enough to know that an intense dislike of pirates—especially singing pirates, which, luckily, are rare—had taken root in the child, and for good reason, too.)

But alas, there would be no swashbuckling today. The sails had gone slack, and the disappointed girl slumped in one of the cozy nursery chairs and clicked idly at the beads of her abacus: back and forth, back and forth.

Penelope noted the changed mood of her three students with dismay. Already she regretted closing the windows. She had done so to make a point about safety, of course, but upon reflection, perhaps a word of caution to Beowulf might have served just as well. For when the windows were open, the children had been happily engaged in educational pursuits: Beowulf was bird-watching, Alexander was navigating, and Cassiopeia had been making colorful threats against unseen pirates, which was good exercise for the imagination, not to mention the girl's rapidly growing vocabulary ("I'll fillet you like a mackerel, *woof!*" had been one of the choicer examples.)

But now the three Incorrigible children were cross and at loose ends, a dangerous combination that could easily tempt any young person to misbehave, never mind three siblings who had been raised in a forest by wolves, and were thus especially prone to mischief.

There was a *tap-tap-tapping* at the window. It was Nutsawoo, the bold gray squirrel whom the children had improbably made into a pet. The furry scamp lived outside in the trees, as any sensible squirrel should, but he had become so tame that he often scurried along a low-hanging branch and made the heroic leap to the windowsill, whereupon Cassiopeia would spoil him with treats and try to teach him to do simple arithmetic with the acorns she had saved expressly for that purpose. Now the bewildered rodent could do nothing but press his nose against the glass and knock with his tiny, monkeylike paws, as his bushy tail flicked to and fro with anxiety.

No one dared get up to open the window, of course. But the reproachful sound could not be ignored. There it was: the *tap-tap-tapping* of a single, sad-eyed, snack-seeking squirrel.

Tap. Tap-tap. Tap-tap-tap. Tap-tap-tap-tap.

If you have ever sniffed at the spout of a carton of milk to judge whether the contents were drinkable, and then found yourself wondering if milk actually goes from fresh to sour all at once in a great curdling swoop, or whether it turns bit by bit, in little souring steps, and if so, at what point along the way the sourness would become evident to the human nose and whether it might not be wiser to simply have a glass of lemonade instead, then you will have some idea of Penelope's current predicament. By now she understood that the mood in the nursery had begun to curdle, so to speak, and that the cause had something to do with her shutting of the windows. However, she was not exactly sure how things had gone so wrong, so quickly. Nor did she know if the morning was already ruined, or if there was yet hope of turning things 'round.

Penelope frowned and drummed her fingers on the cover of her book. It was not quite a year since she had become governess to the Incorrigibles. All three of the children had made remarkable strides regarding their own educations, yet there were many times that their governess felt she was still figuring things out "on the fly," so to speak. This was one of those times.

"Would anyone like to be quizzed on Latin verbs?" she suggested, half-heartedly.

The children shook their heads and sighed. Beowulf had given up building towers and was now gnawing on the blocks. Alexander idly poked his sister with the sextant, and Cassiopeia clutched her abacus in a way that suggested it might soon be hurled across the room.

"What shall I do?" Penelope thought, for she recognized a looming disaster when she saw one. "Ought I reopen the windows and risk appearing foolish, as I have only just closed them? Or should I leave them shut and try to jolly up the children some other way? Perhaps they would like me to read to them. . . ."

But then she felt a sharp pang of guilt, for Penelope knew that the reason she had taken her eyes off Beowulf to begin with was that she had reached a particularly exciting part of the very book she now held in her hands, and as a result had temporarily forgotten—just for a moment, of course—that she was a governess in a nursery at all.

The volume in question was one of the Giddy-Yap, Rainbow! series that Penelope was so fond of. In it, the tale's heroine, Edith-Anne Pevington, enters her trusty pony, Rainbow, in a pony-and-rider show. Once there, a comical mix-up involving lookalike saddles causes Edith-Anne to meet a boy named Albert, who also plans to take part in the show. His dappled pony, Starburst, is as spirited and high-strung as Rainbow is gentle and sweet.

The confusion about the saddles is quickly settled, but the encounter with Albert leaves Edith-Anne flummoxed and unable to do anything but braid and rebraid Rainbow's already perfectly groomed mane and tail, if only to keep her mind off this distracting new acquaintance. *Rainbow in Ribbons* was the title of the book, and the pony show was the centerpiece of the plot, but this sideline business with Albert had captured Penelope's imagination in a way that made the book strangely difficult to put down, even when her own, real-life pupils were climbing out of windows and so forth. For Albert reminded her of a recent acquaintance of her own—a perfectly nice young man named Simon Harley-Dickinson, whom she had met in London, and was not certain when she might see again. . . .

"It *was* a warbler," Cassiopeia muttered to Beowulf, as she fended off Alexander with her abacus. "Stop drooling and draw it."

Somewhat cheered, Beowulf turned away from chewing his blocks and took out his sketchbook. "For the guidebook," he announced, and got to work.

The word "guidebook" made Penelope feel yet another, different sort of pang—not only because she herself had recently lost a rather unusual guidebook which had been given to her as a gift (more about that later)—but because Penelope had given the children an assignment to make a guidebook of their own, and this, too, was proving problematic.

The book was to be called *Birds of Ashton Place, as Seen from the Nursery Window*, but after three days of diligent bird-watching, even Penelope had to admit that only the most common and frankly uninteresting birds were so unimaginative as to spend their days lingering close to the house. Nuthatches, warblers, sparrows, and the occasional wood-dove—perfectly acceptable birds all, to be sure, but where were the sage and mysterious owls? The soaring red kites, with their broad and tireless wings? Or the peregrine falcons, with their blade-like talons and darting eyes that could spot a tasty field mouse on the ground from hundreds of feet in the air?

Clearly, none of these noble specimens was likely to make an appearance at the nursery window, and even the everyday birds refused to hold still long enough for the children to get a proper look at them. Beowulf's near-leap after the nuthatch (or, more likely, warbler) had made the limitations of Penelope's plan all too clear. Yet bringing these three half-tamed, wolf-raised children outside, into the woods—surely that would be unwise? For who was to say how they would behave, if they wandered too far from the house?

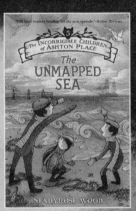